I0847352

Sarita Dasgupta is a writer, editor, poet, playwright, and dedicated tea drinker.

Sarita spent most of her life in the state of Assam (India) amidst acres of green tea bushes, where she developed a deep and abiding love and respect for Nature and the many wild creatures she encountered. Her previously published works - *Feathered Friends* - a collection of fables for children - has birds as characters. Her two series of English Literature and Language textbooks for schoolchildren - *Rainbow Reader* and *The Tree of Knowledge* - contain original stories, poems and essays focused on respect for animals and the environment among other relevant issues.

The seven stories in this book are all works of fiction, springing from the author's imagination, though partly inspired by her own and others' experiences in the unique world of tea.

Sarita spent eleven creatively fulfilling years as Editor of a multi-national tea company's corporate magazine. She contributes articles to a blog spot dedicated to life and experiences on tea estates around the world.

This book is for my husband, Chris.

GEKKER PUBLISHING

Copyright © 2024 by Sarita Dasgupta

Published 2024 by Gekker Publishing

http://gekkerpublishing.com

Seattle, WA 98118

First Edition

Printed in the United States

Logo design by Rachel Kotkin

Cover art © 2024 by Rachel Kotkin

Seeds of Fate is a work of fiction. Any resemblance to actual
events, places, incidents, person or persons living or dead,
is completely coincidental.

ISBN-13: 979-8-9918840-9-9

Seeds of Fate

by Sarita Dasgupta

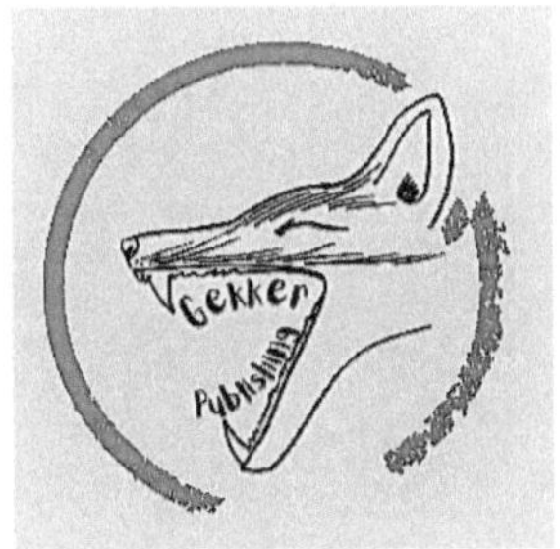

Contents

Seeds of Fate

The seeds of Fate are sown in the past

but bear fruit in the future.

Brinda sat on the verandah of her little cottage and watched the mist slowly disappear as the sun grew brighter. She kept her mobile phone close by because she knew that calls from her family and friends would start coming in very soon. Trying to distract her mind, she looked at the beautifully laid out flower beds in the garden below, and thought again how fortunate she had been to find Robi, not only because he was a dedicated gardener with green fingers but also because he was from Assam where she had spent most of her life.

He had started working at the guest house almost a year ago. When she had spoken to him in Assamese, he had been taken aback but had quickly recovered and replied in the same language.

He had explained that his two older brothers worked for a security firm in Pune and had asked him to join them. However, he was more interested in gardening and had heard that Mahabaleshwar had beautiful flowers growing throughout the year, so he had decided to try his luck there.

"But why did you leave Assam?" she had asked.

He had looked away and mumbled, "There is nothing for me there."

She had told him that she would take him on for a trial period of three months in which time he could also decide whether or not the job suited him. He had turned out to be extremely hardworking and an excellent gardener. The flower beds were always full of blooms and the kitchen had a steady supply of fresh herbs, papayas, and some seasonal vegetables. She had offered to hire someone to help him but he had declined. She had observed the way he nurtured the plants – gently and lovingly. "As if they're his children," she had thought. "Perhaps he doesn't want anyone else touching them in case they handle them roughly and damage them." Although Robi was practical about the herbs, fruit and vegetables, he hated cutting even a single flower. She thought how fortunate she was to have found such a gem of a gardener for the guest house.

She sipped her tea and looked up at the hills across the shimmering lake as they were slowly bathed in the early morning light. "Nothing can compare to Nature's beauty," she thought, "and nothing can compare to Man's inhumanity!" She shivered and pulled her shawl tighter around her.

***

Ten years ago, Brinda's husband, Pradeep, had been kidnapped by militants just a kilometer from the gates of the tea estate he managed in Assam when he was returning from a meeting one evening. Ironically, the meeting had been called by the District Commissioner to discuss the growing activities of the militants, and the precautions that potential targets needed to take! While the tea company Pradeep worked for, and the police, were trying to secure his release, his body, with the fatal bullet wound in the back, had been left outside the local police station in the dead of night. According to a press release by the high-profile militant group, he had died in an "accident." All she could remember was being told by their friend, Surinder, that Pradeep was dead. Everything that had come after seemed to be shrouded in a dense cloud in her mind.

"At least the body has been returned for the last rites, thank God!" she had heard someone comment. Then, it hadn't made much of an impact but later, she realized that the militants could have quietly disposed of Pradeep's body and she would never have known whether he was still alive or dead. Shuddering, she wondered how long she would have been able to cope, seesawing between hope and despair.

She never knew how he had come to be shot in the back by "accident" but their friends as well as the media believed that he had been shot while trying to escape. Surinder's wife, Kiran, had said, "He must have been desperate to come back to you."

"Desperate to come back to his liquor, more likely," had been the unbidden thought that had come into her still-stunned mind, only to be hastily erased.

She thought of the innumerable club events and parties over the last year... how she had dreaded them! Pradeep, the loving husband, cheerful friend and dignified "Burra Sahab" would turn into someone quite different after a few drinks. There he would be, arguing loudly in slurred tones, swaying his way to the buffet table, more often than not dropping his fork if not the whole plate of food. And she would smile and smile, holding on to the shreds of her pride. Their friends would make a joke of it and bundle him into the back seat of the car while she thanked the hosts and tried to make as dignified an exit as possible. On the drive home, she would feel something akin to hate for the man snoring beside her. When they got home, their driver and the night watchman would silently help Pradeep get out of the car and into the bedroom. They would bid her goodnight respectfully and leave the room with downcast eyes, while Brinda tried not to show her embarrassment. The next day, however, Pradeep would be his usual self and she couldn't help loving him.

She had tried to talk to him about his drinking and explain how humiliating his behavior was for both of them. He would promise to give it up but forget as soon as he came home in the evening. He had started drinking every evening while she had been away in Los Angeles for a month the previous year, looking after her niece while her sister was recuperating after an operation. That had been the longest that she and Pradeep had been apart since they were married. By the time she had returned, his daily drinking was an established routine. When she had tried to remonstrate, it had led to a huge fight culminating in her threat to leave him. He had looked at her levelly and said, "Then go!" The next day, of course, he had apologized and become quite emotional. "It's this job," he'd explained. "There's so much stress. Not only the pressures that come with the job, but external factors like this insurgency problem…You weren't here to talk to, and I needed to de-stress. Try to understand, sweetheart."

"But I'm back now, and I'm not going anywhere," she'd said. He'd patted her shoulder affectionately and left for work, but that evening, the glass of amber fluid was back in his hand. Brinda had seriously considered her options, although she knew she didn't really have any. As she had married Pradeep straight after her Class 12 examinations, she had neither the qualifications nor the experience to get a job. Deep down, she knew she lacked the confidence to be on her own. She also knew that left on his own, Pradeep would just go from bad to worse. After all, hadn't that been the very reason why he had started drinking while she'd been away? Out of loneliness? She loved him too much to leave him and risk his becoming an alcoholic. She had tried her best to control his alcohol intake as much as possible, incurring his wrath in the process. Despite the deep love between them, their relationship had been very strained when he had been kidnapped but no one would have guessed. She had held up appearances to the last.

But after his tragic death, all the unpleasantness of that last year was forgotten. She could only remember how much they had loved each other, and her heart wrenched with the realization that she would never, ever, see him again, or hear his voice, or feel his touch. While she moved around in a fog, haunted by the horror of Pradeep's violent death, waking drenched with sweat from nightmares in the wee hours, Surinder, and Pradeep's other colleagues, organized everything – the cremation, the *"Shraddh"* ceremony and the other rites. Pradeep's younger brother, Preetam, came from Mumbai and performed the last rites, as she and Pradeep didn't have any children. "Thank God my parents aren't alive today. They couldn't have borne such a terrible loss," Brinda heard Preetam say to Surinder out on the verandah. "When I think of my brother being shot in the back..." he shook his head, unable to express his anger and sorrow.

Surinder squeezed his shoulder in sympathy. "I hope his murderer is caught and punished. He should hang," he said with quiet fury.

"Or be shot dead," said Preetam.

"Yes, that might happen," said Surinder, "either in the hands of the police or his own comrades. There's been quite a hue and cry by the local people who liked and respected Pradeep very much. Many local politicians, businessmen, student leaders and the media have added their voices to the tea community's, condemning Pradeep's murder, and demanding that the persons responsible for it be brought to justice."

"But why did they choose to kidnap my brother in particular?" asked Preetam.

"I don't think it was that. They were just looking for an opportunity to pick up any tea planter of a certain seniority and hold him for ransom, trying to force the Company to pay," explained Surinder.

Brinda moved away, thinking, "So it was sheer bad luck that they picked up my Pradeep!" She pressed her hands to her mouth to hold back her agonized sobs.

After the "*Shraddh*," Preetam had to return to Mumbai, but planned to come back when Brinda was ready to leave. He was worried about leaving her on her own, but Surinder reassured him, saying, "Don't worry. We are all here for her. Kiran and another friend, Devika, will stay with her, and supervise the packing,"

"Thank you. I'm relieved to know that. My wife can't come because of our two-year-old son, and I came in a hurry, so I have to go back and organize a few things at work. Brinda's parents are in the US with her sister. They were shocked and distressed but after discussing it with Brinda, I told them not to return. As soon as everything is settled, she can join them in Los Angeles," he explained. "Please keep in touch and let me know when she's ready to leave," he added.

Surinder reassured him again, but Preetam had a hard time taking his leave of Brinda. What he didn't know was that she was relieved to see him go. When Pradeep was alive, she had never realized how similar the two brothers were. Now, her heart skipped a beat every time she heard Preetam speak. The voices were different but the cadences were similar. Certain expressions, gestures, and even the walk, were very similar. It was bittersweet but disturbing at the same time. She hoped that, in time, it would stop bothering her, but for the moment, she couldn't cope with these constant reminders. The fog in her mind was suddenly penetrated with the realization that Preetam had lost his brother; his only sibling, whom he had loved and looked up to. She didn't know what to say but hugged him hoping he would understand. He had hugged her back and given her a ghost of his usual lopsided smile. "How lucky I am to have a brother-in-law like Preetam!" she thought fondly. She was glad he didn't know about Pradeep's drinking and his embarrassing behavior in the last year.

She pulled herself together to identify what she needed and what she didn't, so that the packers could do the needful. The Company had been kind, and told Brinda to take all the time she needed, but Brinda wanted to leave as soon as possible. She had always loved her life in Assam, but now she just wanted to get away. Every time the gate opened and a vehicle entered the driveway, she imagined it was Pradeep returning home. There were too many reminders of him around the bungalow. She doubted she could hold on to her control if she had to stay there much longer.

Preetam was in constant touch with Surinder, and organized the transfer of her belongings to her apartment in Kolkata. Between him and Surinder, they had taken care of everything while she just coasted along. She was very grateful to them both and also to Kiran, Devika and all her other friends. She realized how true it was that the tea planters' community rallied around one of their own in times of need.

Everyone had been so sympathetic and helpful. All the staff and workers on the estate came to bid her farewell and Pradeep's colleagues went to the airport to see her and Preetam off. She was touched by their kindness. On the flight to Kolkata, she looked with tearful eyes and heavy heart at the disappearing tea bushes below and was overcome by the sense of finality – Pradeep was gone forever and so was her life in the tea estates of Assam. It was the only life she had known as her father had also been a tea planter.

Preetam and Brinda spent a week in Kolkata doing all the necessary paperwork regarding Pradeep's benefits from the Company, his bank accounts and investments. Although everyone was very kind and helpful, Brinda didn't know what she would have done without Preetam. She was finding it really difficult to concentrate on anything for more than a few minutes at a time. She couldn't free her mind from images of Pradeep being shot and falling dead. So lost was she in her own thoughts that she didn't notice the concerned looks that Preetam darted at her from time to time. He spoke to his wife Deepa, who was equally concerned.

After completing all the formalities, Brinda and Preetam locked up her flat and flew to Mumbai. There, two-year-old Rahul's antics took her mind off her grief for brief periods, but she seemed to be growing more and more silent. Deepa then decided to tackle the problem head on. She spoke gently to Brinda, suggesting that she talk to a counselor. "Brin, you need to talk your heart out to someone who's not family." At first, Brinda had demurred but at Deepa's affectionate insistence, agreed to see the counselor Deepa's doctor had recommended.

At first, she had been unable to open up but the counselor had been so patient, sympathetic and non-judgmental, that she had felt a growing sense of comfort. "Although I grieve for Pradeep, part of me was relieved to be free of the constant unpleasantness and stress of the last year. I suppose this makes me feel guilty. And the fact that I had thought of leaving him," she told the counselor.

"Listen, every marriage goes through its ups and downs, with spouses threatening to leave, or at least contemplating it. It's quite common," the counselor had assured her.

"I should remember the many good years we had together, and how loving he was," said Brinda.

"Yes, dwell on the happy memories," agreed the counselor.

"But what do I do about the nightmares?" asked Brinda quietly. "I can't get over the way he died. I'm filled with such rage…"

"Talk about it, Brinda. Express your sorrow and rage. Don't bottle it up," advised the counselor.

At the end of a month, Brinda realized what a good decision going to the counselor had been. She felt much lighter and better able to deal with her loss, and also with the guilt she felt at having even contemplated leaving Pradeep. Even when she was in Los Angeles, surrounded by the loving comfort of her parents, sister, brother-in-law and little niece, she kept in touch with her counselor.

After returning to India, the thought of being on her own after living with someone, and being emotionally dependent on him for twenty years, terrified her.

She knew that she would be all right financially. She was not an extravagant person. She would live carefully. Much to her surprise, however, soon after she returned from USA, she was offered a job by Manav, a friend of Preetam's, who owned a small guest house in Mahabaleshwar, a hill station a few hours' drive from Mumbai. "Is he doing this as a favor to you or because he feels sorry for me?" she asked Preetam.

"Neither," was Preetam's reply. "He stayed with you and Pradeep in Assam for a few days, remember? He was really impressed with your skills as a hostess, and thinks you are just the person he's looking for. It's a small, homelike place, with only ten rooms. Manav has a chap who looks after the bookings, billing and the finances. He wants you to look after the rooms, the food, and the garden, and manage the staff. You know, the housekeeping part."

Deepa encouraged her to take it, saying, "You kept a beautiful home and know how to manage household staff. You can make menus for every meal without giving it much thought. Come on, you can do this with your eyes shut, Brin! And Mahabaleshwar's just a few hours away from us. You can come here when you crave the bright lights and we can come to you when we want to run away from them!"

Preetam had added, "Give it a try, Brin. You can leave if you don't like it."

"But I don't have any qualifications…" she began saying but Preetam cut her short. "Listen Brin. I work in HR so I know that qualifications don't always reflect a person's abilities. Manav's years of experience have taught him this too. You have skills and abilities that were honed over two decades of experience. You are efficient and organized. It's just that no one gave you a certificate validating your skills. Come on, I've never seen you lack confidence in dealing with anyone – from VIPs to your household staff. So, what's the problem?"

"That was in my own home and my own, familiar, world, Preetam. I don't know if I have the courage…"

Brinda was cut short again by Preetam, who exclaimed with disbelief, "You don't know if you have the courage! Good God, Brin. Look at the way in which you've dealt with Pradeep's death! That's called quiet courage. Courage isn't always flamboyant, you know. Just living from one day to the next after a loss like yours, with the dignity you've shown, takes courage. So, stop talking rot, and take up Manav's offer. It's a job that's tailor-made for you. Discuss it with your parents and your friend, Kiran. I'm sure they'll agree with me."

"But what about my apartment in Kolkata?" asked Brinda.

"We'll find you a reliable tenant," said Preetam. He spoke to a friend in Kolkata who contacted a broker. Within a fortnight, a tenant had been found.

"So, now are you ready to take on the job?" asked Preetam.

"I…I…think so," replied Brinda hesitantly. Seeing Preetam's reproving look, she hastily added, "Okay, okay, I don't need another morale-boosting lecture. I'm ready to go to Mahabaleshwar and start the next chapter of my life."

"That's good to hear," said Preetam, "because I've already told Manav we'll drive up on Saturday!"

Brinda gave him an outraged look but he just grinned and left the room. Deepa came up to her and gave her a hug. "It'll be fine, you'll see," she said reassuringly.

That had been almost ten years ago. She had loved the quaint guest house and the garden with its profusion of flowers. Her little cottage on a promontory in a corner of the property was reminiscent of the smaller bungalows that she and Pradeep had lived in while he was still an Assistant Manager. She had settled in comfortably and found that, just as Preetam and Deepa had assured her, running the guest house was very much like running her home in Assam and looking after Company guests, who had mostly been strangers too. Soon, the same people kept coming back and recommending the guest house to friends. Her homemade strawberry jam, cupcakes and brownies, trifle pudding and all the other dishes she had learned to make while in the tea estates, and which she had taught the cooks in the guest house, were big hits with the guests. She was happy and proud when Manav told her that she was excellent at her job. He raised her salary and when she demurred, he said, "Listen, Brinda. The guest house is doing well because of you. You are marvelous with people. You have the personal touch. The guests come back because of you, your great menus, and your homemade delicacies! As for the staff, I don't think I could have kept the same ones on for all these years if not for you. Do you think I'm going to risk losing you to some other place?"

Astonished, she said, "But I wouldn't dream of leaving! I love it here."

"I'm relieved to know that," grinned Manav, "but you deserve a raise anyway." For an infinitesimal moment, his eyes softened as they rested on her happy face, then he went on to discuss work in his usual brisk manner.

As she had got to know Manav, she had come to appreciate his business acumen and his integrity. She had also realized that under that practical demeanor lurked a very kind heart. One day, while talking to him, she absentmindedly noticed the grooves on his cheeks when he smiled, and the way his hair touched the collar of his shirt. She thought fondly that he really needed a good haircut and some new clothes. She impulsively told him this, and he actually blushed! She hastily apologized but on his next visit, she noticed that his hair was cut professionally and he was wearing very smart khaki Chinos with a checked shirt, corduroy jacket and loafers. She complimented him most sincerely and he seemed pleased though slightly embarrassed.

He had made it clear that her personal guests, such as her family members and close friends, were welcome to stay free of cost. Her parents had come twice in the last ten years, her sister and family once, and Kiran and Surinder once. Preetam, Deepa and Rahul came very often so they insisted on paying, but Manav gave them the "family discount."

In the idyllic surroundings, Brinda found it easier and easier to remember all the good things in their marriage as the months passed, but this made her miss Pradeep even more. She discovered that she could express her deepest feelings and thoughts in verse. Writing them down was cathartic and made her feel more at peace. She had slowly come to terms with her loss but was still anguished by the violent way in which Pradeep had died and the fact that his murderer was still unknown and unpunished as far as anyone knew. She sometimes had sleepless nights, and it was on such nights that she sat and expressed her feelings in verse. Last night, on the eve of Pradeep's tenth death anniversary, she had composed a poem called "Reminders of You." She wondered if she would ever share her poetry with anyone. They somehow seemed too personal. Moreover, her parents, sister, Preetam and Deepa had all suggested gently, in their own way, that she should try and move on.

Deepa and Preetam had not missed the softness in the fleeting looks Manav unwittingly sent in Brinda's direction. They realized that although Brinda seemed fond of Manav and enjoyed his company, she was quite oblivious to his feelings, still wrapped up as she was in her grief.

"It's because she hasn't got closure," said Deepa. "Pradeep's murderer is still out there as far as we know."

Preetam nodded in agreement. "It's a pity. I can't think of a better guy for her than Manav, though" he said. "I hope she sees that for herself, and soon."

At their next meeting, he gently told Brinda, "Keep an open mind about finding someone new, Brin. You're only in your forties… still a young woman."

Brinda had pretended to agree but she believed that she'd never find another "kindred spirit" like Pradeep.

Her mind went back to her first meeting with Pradeep. She was home from her boarding school after her Class 10 Board examinations, and had a few months' holiday to look forward to before she joined Junior College. Pradeep was her father's new Assistant Manager. She was sixteen, he was twenty-three. For her, it had been "love at first sight," but he hadn't shown much interest in her at first. They partnered each other on the tennis court at their local club, and she wheedled him to teach her golf so that she could spend hours with him on the 18-hole golf course on Sundays. "Only if your parents give their permission," he had said.

Her father was rather surprised at her sudden interest in golf. "I thought you said it was too slow for you, and you preferred to run about on the tennis court," he had commented with a raised eyebrow.

"Oh, I've changed my mind," she'd replied airily. Her father looked at her mother enquiringly. "What do you think?"

"Golf will teach her patience and discipline. As long as Pradeep doesn't mind, though."

"He doesn't," she assured them quickly.

Walking out of the dining room, Brinda froze as she heard her mother say, "You do realize Brinda has a crush on Pradeep, don't you?"

"Yes. I suppose it's only natural. He's handsome, intelligent, and a good sportsman," her father replied. "But don't worry, we can trust him with her."

"I'm sure we can," said her mother, "otherwise I wouldn't have agreed."

Ears burning, Brinda stalked off to her room. "Am I that transparent?" she asked herself. "Oh no! Does Pradeep also realize I have a crush on him?" She was mortified. The next time they met, she was rather cool and cast oblique looks at him to see his reaction. He treated her with the same polite friendliness, so she concluded that he hadn't guessed. "My parents have said you can teach me to play golf, as long as you don't mind. You don't, do you?" she asked him anxiously.

"No, that's fine. Your dad told me. I hope you're serious, though. I don't want to waste my time."

"Oh yes, I'm serious," she assured him.

"That's fine, then," he said. "We'll start next Sunday. I'll pick you up at 7 AM."

"Seven o'clock in the morning? On a Sunday?" she asked in dismay.

"Yes. Please be ready on time," he said.

"Yes sir," she muttered under her breath, throwing a mock salute at his departing back.

"Where did you learn to play golf so well?" she asked him. "At the Army golf course in Pune," he replied, "when my dad was posted there. When he moved away, my brother and I became boarders at The Bishop's School. There was always a friend of my father's posted in Pune at any given time, who became our 'local guardian,' so we got to play golf on Saturday mornings when we were allowed to go out, and during short holidays."

"So, your father is an army officer?" she asked.

"Yes," he replied. "He's in the army engineers. He's a Major General."

"Wow! That's impressive," she commented. He slanted her a smile.

"Where are your parents now?" she asked.

"Back in Pune," he replied. "They're planning to settle down there after retirement."

"Oh, okay. Does your mother work?" she asked.

"No, she's an army wife. Like your mother, she goes with Dad wherever he's posted. But she's very involved in the welfare of army widows and children, just like your mother gets involved in the welfare of the tea estate workers and their children. Actually, our mothers are quite similar. Both elegant, efficient, well read, well spoken, and kind-hearted. They would have been assets to any company or institution they'd worked for," he said.

"Instead, they married a tea planter and army officer respectively, both involving frequent transfers and postings in remote areas," she said.

"Yes. My parents couldn't imagine living apart, except when he was posted in non-family stations," he added.

"Living apart was never an option for my parents either," said Brinda.

They smiled at each other, sharing the confidence that comes from having parents who so obviously loved each other and their children.

"Pradeep is so handsome!" she wrote in a letter to her younger sister who was away at boarding school, "but doesn't seem to realize it." Her sister was her best friend and confidante. "He is the 'complete package,' yet not at all conceited." She went on to describe his various talents and virtues at such length that her sister wrote back asking if he was real! Brinda was indignant but smiled sheepishly when she read the "rough copy" of her own letter again. She *had* gone on a bit!

She and Pradeep slowly got to know each other over the next few months, and soon Pradeep was as besotted, much as he told himself, and her, that she was "just a kid." "I never thought I'd fall in love with a teenager!" he told her.

"You talk like you're my grandfather!" she exclaimed. "You're only seven years older. That may seem like a lot now, but after a few years it won't matter."

"I suppose so, but it matters now. You're only sixteen!"

"But you love me! I still can't believe it," she said. Looking up into his eyes, she put her arms around his neck.

He hugged her hard then released her. "Don't do that, Brinda. It's hard for me. Your parents trust me to be the gentleman with you. I can't betray that trust. Besides, you aren't an adult yet."

"An officer and a gentleman," she teased.

"Yes," he said seriously, "Just as I was brought up to be."

When she finished Junior College after two years, Pradeep asked her father for permission to propose to her. Although her parents liked Pradeep, they felt she was too young to commit to marriage, and wanted her to go to college first. She was adamant and flatly refused to study any further. "What for?" she'd asked. "I'm going to be a tea planter's wife, which, as a tea planter's daughter, I'm fully qualified for."

Finally, her parents had given in, and Pradeep's parents had also agreed. They had always been good to her, she thought fondly now.

They got married and she couldn't have been happier. "Where's that officer and gentleman now?" she'd teased after a very satisfactory bout of lovemaking.

"Right here," he'd replied. "His only duty is to keep his wife happy in every way." When they'd found out that she was pregnant, they'd been ecstatic. But then she miscarried, and the gynecologist asked them to do some tests. She had studied the results and said, "I'm so sorry to have to tell you this, but judging from these test results, it's better if you don't have children together."

Brinda heard a ringing in her ears through which she barely heard Pradeep asking, "What do you mean? Why shouldn't we have children?"

The doctor was explaining about genes and chromosomes but Brinda just shut out the sound of her voice. All she could think was, "Never have a child! We can never have a child!" Suddenly, she asked, "What do you mean by 'together'?"

"I mean that, medically speaking, you can have children with other people but not with each other. But of course, the question doesn't arise, since you are married to each other," the doctor added hastily.

Brinda had brooded over the doctor's words and told Pradeep, "If you want to divorce me and marry someone else, and have children, just tell me."

"What? Are you crazy?" he'd exclaimed. "Of course I don't want to divorce you! I love you. I want to be married to you for the rest of my life." He'd held her tightly while she'd let the tears flow. "Sweetheart, I'm as shattered as you are, but if we shouldn't have children, we have to accept it. You are more than enough for me. In fact, you are everything to me." Later, he told her that the doctor had advised him to have a vasectomy. "It's no big deal.

They'll just tie a tube. I should have it done so that there are no accidental pregnancies."

Over the years, they grew used to being just the two of them. Perhaps it even drew them closer.

***

She was awakened from her reverie by the sound of the garden gate opening below. Looking down, she saw Robi, and called out to him. He looked startled to see her, but mounted the stone steps to her cottage, greeting her respectfully. She thought he looked pale and strained but before she could ask him what the matter was, one of the staff came running to say that she was wanted in the kitchen. Hurrying after him, just as her phone started ringing, she called out to the gardener over her shoulder, "Robi, I know you hate cutting flowers but, just for today, could you please cut some white roses and place them in the vase next to my husband's photograph on the mantelpiece in my drawing room? Thank you."

Robi descended the steps and went to one of the rose bushes, cut six white blooms reluctantly and walked slowly up to Brinda's cottage. He had never been inside before. Hesitantly, he entered the drawing room and looked around. Like a magnet, the photograph on the mantelpiece pulled his reluctant feet forward until he was staring at the smiling face of the only man he had ever killed in his life; ten years ago, on this day. Rooted to the spot, the roses falling from his nerveless hands, he thought he would faint. Then his mind went hurtling back…

***

He was a teenager, frustrated with the endless penury of his days. His father, Laben, eked out a living planting paddy on a small piece of low-lying land which had belonged to his family for generations. He refused to augment his pittance of an income by working as a "laborer" in the neighboring tea estates. As a landowner, he felt it was below his dignity. However, he had no objection to his wife, Meena, working as a plucker on an estate, since the money she brought in enabled him to indulge his drinking and smoking. Robi despised his lazy and unambitious father but loved his mother. If not for her, he would have left home long ago. She had joined the scheme for weavers that the Manager's wife had started on the estate with the Company's help. Women were given thread and designs to take home and weave fabric on their hand looms in their own time. They were paid a reasonable sum for their work, and did not have to worry about the procurement of thread or the sale of the fabric. Meena was full of praise for the kind lady who was trying to help the women on the estate and surrounding villages to earn some extra income for themselves. "The Burra Sahab and Memsahab are both very kind," Meena told Laben and Robi, as she showed them the money she had earned for her weaving. "Huh! It's easy to be kind when you live in a big house filled with servants," scoffed Laben, snatching the notes from her hand.

"Give that back!" she cried. "That money is for Robi's school fees!"

"School fees! Don't encourage that boy to waste his time in school, filling his head with ideas beyond his station in life. He should be working on our paddy fields."

"Yes, I should be working while you lie back, drinking and smoking and wasting Ma's hard-earned money!" exclaimed Robi in disgust.

"Is that what you have learned in school? To speak disrespectfully to your father?" demanded Laben angrily, advancing on Robi menacingly.

"No, I have learned that respect has to be earned, so why don't you earn it, you good-for-nothing drunkard?" shouted Robi, and ran out of the house even as he heard his mother cry, "Robi!" in a distressed tone.

He and his friends always talked about getting away from what they thought of as their dead-end village. "There's nothing for us here. We have to go to a city like Guwahati. That's the kind of life we want. Movie halls, restaurants, all kinds of shops..." Bipin had said.

"Yes, and no money to spend on anything!" Nabin had scoffed.

"We'll have to get jobs, of course," Robi had said.

"Of course! People are just waiting to give us jobs!" Nabin had said sarcastically. "After all, we are better educated and qualified than all the city boys!"

Months later, Robi had realized what easy recruits he and his friends must have been for the militants who were trying to enroll young boys and girls to fill their ranks. Disgruntled teens, looking for some excitement in their humdrum lives and the promise of money…

Along with the other recruits, he was trained in handling a gun. For a teenaged boy, this was the ultimate fantasy come true, till he had to carry the heavy gun and march over rough terrain for hours at a time. After months of tramping through dense forests, sleeping uncomfortably on hard ground while getting bitten by mosquitoes, and eating even more frugal meals than he'd had at home, his enthusiasm for "the cause" was wearing rather thin.

But when he was told to guard the prisoner in a room of the village house they were hiding in, he was proud of having been given such an important job, although he was surprised that the prisoner was never restrained. When he asked one of his comrades why this was so, he was told that they had no enmity towards the prisoner himself. In fact, he was highly respected by the local populace. "We have nothing against him but he represents the Company. We want the Company to pay for his release. Then we'll use the money for our cause. He won't try to escape. Not with at least one gun trained on him at all times."

Robi held his weapon the way he had been taught to, and kept careful watch, but they had trudged a long way through the jungle that day so he was tired and must have fallen asleep late at night. Suddenly, a slight sound woke him. Jerking up he saw the prisoner walking out of the door! Aghast and fearing the punishment he would face if he allowed the prisoner to escape, he shouted, "Stop, or I'll fire!" The man stopped and was turning around to tell him something but in his befuddled and nervous state, Robi's finger had pressed the trigger and the next thing he knew, the man had fallen face down on the floor.

Hearing the shot, the others had woken up and come rushing towards the room. But Robi hadn't waited. He had jumped out of the window, and run… and run…and run…

***

After years spent hiding from his erstwhile comrades who had faced a great deal of negative publicity after the prisoner's death, he had landed up in Mahabaleshwar where he had put his heart and soul into gardening. Perhaps giving life to plants and nurturing them had been his way of atoning for the life he had taken.

Now, he thought of Brinda who had been so kind to him, and a strangled cry of agony left his lips. He heard footsteps approaching the cottage. Bolting out of the drawing room, he came face to face with a startled Brinda. He stared at her with agonized eyes, his slack lips trying to form some sort of apology, but words failed him. Looking away in terror and shame, he bolted down the steps, and just ran…and ran…and ran… while Brinda stood frozen on the verandah, knowing intuitively that she had just come face to face with her husband's killer…

Watching the running figure grow smaller and smaller before disappearing from view, she felt the heaviness around her heart fall away at last.

There was no need to punish her husband's killer… because he was already in hell.

An Accidental Meeting

We meet people not by chance, but by Fate's design.

Captain Charles Wentworth of the Royal Navy looked at his watch. He was back at Dartmouth, Devon, for his class reunion at the Naval Academy that he had graduated from more than two decades ago. He had enjoyed the break spent catching up with his classmates, some of whom he hadn't seen since leaving the Academy. It was interesting to hear about their experiences since then. Just relaxing and enjoying the company of old friends had taken his mind off the task that lay ahead.

"Hey, Charlie! That's the third time you looked at your watch in the last five minutes!" cried Tom Pritchard, "I know we're boring old men now, but really, are we that bad?"

Charles smiled and said, "You'll never be boring, Tom. You were always the prankster. I'll bet you drive your wife up the wall!"

Tom grinned and said, "She never knows who's going to come through the door at the end of the day. The many moods and faces of Tom Pritchard. It spices up our lives."

Everyone laughed and the talk turned general. Charles sat quietly, letting the atmosphere of bonhomie and camaraderie wash over him for a few minutes, then he stood up and announced that he had to leave.

"See, I told you, he finds us boring," said Tom with a mock scowl.

"Actually, I have to get back to my ship and hand over charge before going on leave," explained Charles.

"Oh, right. Going anywhere interesting?" asked Monty Bell.

"Uh, yes, you could say so," replied Charles. "I'm going to India."

"Ah!" exclaimed Monty. "Exotic! Have you been there before?"

Charles hesitated, then said, "Yes, but I was very young, so I don't remember anything."

"Family going with you?" asked Monty.

"No, I'm going alone," replied Charles shortly. He didn't explain that he was divorced and that his daughter, Charlotte, was studying in France.

"Enough with the inquisition, Monty," said Tom. "Well, bon voyage Charlie boy!" he added.

"Thanks, Tom," said Charles, and went around the table shaking hands and saying "goodbye" to his classmates.

Driving on the A38 to HMNB Devonport where his ship was docked, Charles switched on the radio which was permanently set to his favorite station, 102.2 Jazz FM. He let the music wash over him, emptying his mind of thought.

It took him less than an hour to reach his ship but the drive and the music had calmed his mind. He called Lieutenant Commander Robert Dexter to his cabin and they spent the next hour discussing what the latter had to do in Charles' absence. Charles had every respect for Robert as an officer and liked him very much as a person. Once all the points had been thoroughly covered, Charles asked his steward to bring them some tea and biscuits. Sipping his cup of Assam tea appreciatively, Charles said, "My father worked all his life for a tea company in Assam, you know."

"Oh, I didn't know that," commented Robert, "although you had mentioned that he'd spent his life in India."

"Yes," said Charles. "He was a tea planter. He was interviewed at the company's London office and offered a job as an Assistant Manager in one of their tea estates in Assam. So off he sailed to lands unknown at the age of twenty. Fortunately, he liked the job and settled down quite well. When he came back to England on leave after a few years, he married my mother and took her back with him. I was born in Calcutta two years later."

"Oh, so you were born in India," said Robert.

"Yes, I was," said Charles. "But my mother just couldn't settle down in Assam. She couldn't handle the heat, the mosquitoes, the language. She was also terrified of losing me to some tropical disease. She tried to stick it out, but gave up and returned to England when I was two. She divorced my father and, after a few years, met and married my step-father."

"Admiral Sir Benedict Rawlings," said Robert.

"Yes," agreed Charles. "I am fortunate to have him as my step-father. But although I didn't meet my own father often, he remained part of my life too. He wrote to me regularly and spent time with me when he came to England on leave."

"Did you ever visit him in India?" asked Robert.

"No, my mother's paranoia hadn't abated one jot, and Dad didn't want to upset her, so he never asked me to go to him," explained Charles.

"What about when you were older?" asked Robert.

"The time just never seemed right. When I had holidays, Dad was busy, so he wouldn't have been able to spend time with me. And then the years just passed, and he retired and came back to England."

"So, you were able to spend time with him when he returned," observed Robert. "Yes," said Charles. "I'm glad we had those years together. He was an interesting man and very good company. He adored Charlotte. But now he's gone and his last wish was that I take his ashes to Assam and scatter them in the Brahmaputra River."

"I see, so that's the reason you're going to India after all these years," said Robert.

"Yes," said Charles. "It's the last thing I can do for my father. I can't deny I'm a little nervous about going to a country I don't know, to fulfil my father's last wish, but I looked it up. The Brahmaputra flows through the breadth of Assam, so I can do it in Guwahati which is well connected by air from New Delhi. I'll fly from Heathrow to New Delhi, spend a couple of days there, and then fly to Guwahati. It wasn't at all difficult doing all the bookings online and over the phone. Flights, hotels and transport, everything."

"Do you know anyone there?" asked Robert.

"No, not a soul," replied Charles, "but the guest house I've booked in Guwahati has a caretaker who can help me with the immersion of the ashes. The owner told me it wouldn't be a problem."

They were silent for a while, then Robert asked, "Did your father never remarry?" "No," replied Charles shortly.

"Is your mother worried about your going?" asked Robert.

"Oh no, she finally realizes that things have changed there since I was two years old!" laughed Charles.

Two days later, Charles took a flight from Heathrow to New Delhi. A car was waiting at the airport to take him to his hotel. The next day, the driver took him sightseeing around the city. He was impressed with the wide roads and historic monuments, and took a whole lot of photographs to send Charlotte. He wanted to pick up a few gifts so the driver took him to Dilli Haat, an open-air market with stalls selling food, clothes and artefacts. He picked up a statue of Ganesh, the elephant-headed god for himself, a dagger with an intricately carved sheath for his step-father, a bamboo flute for Pat, and colorful scarves for his mother and Charlotte. As he was leaving the stall, he bumped into someone coming in. He apologized, but the other man smiled and said, "That's all right."

As Charles walked away, the stranger looked back at Charles in a puzzled manner. Then he shook his head and entered the stall.

Charles sat under a colorful umbrella and sipped a refreshing cup of Assam tea as he lazily watched people moving around Dilli Haat. He saw the man whom he had bumped into earlier, come out of the shop speaking on his mobile phone. He sat under another umbrella, and glancing at Charles, nodded politely. Charles smiled briefly and nodded back. He finished his tea, paid his bill and got up to leave. Just then his mobile rang, and he saw that the call was from Charlotte.

"Hello, Darling!" he said. Charlotte fired a whole lot of questions at him, to which he laughingly replied, "Hold on, hold on! Give me a chance to answer one question before you fire the next, Sweetheart!" He started walking towards the exit. Suddenly someone called, "Excuse me."

Turning around, Charles saw the same gentlemen he had bumped into, holding out his shopping bag.

"You left this behind," he said.

Charles told Charlotte he'd call her back and put away his phone.

He took the bag from the other man and said gratefully, "Thank you very much. The phone call must have distracted me."

The other man smiled and said, "I'm glad I saw it before you left." He looked at Charles searchingly and asked, "Have we met before?"

Charles said, "I don't think so."

The man shook his head. "Perhaps it's just that you look familiar. I'm Naveen Dutta," he said, holding out his hand.

Charles shook his hand and said, "Pleased to meet you. I'm Charles Wentworth." Naveen's hand froze in Charles'. "Is there something wrong?" Charles asked.

"No, no. I'm just surprised. Are you related to Mr. Gilbert Wentworth?"

"Yes, he was my father. Did you know him?" asked Charles surprised.

Naveen nodded, saying, "A legendary tea planter and an inspiration to me and many other planters. You look a lot like him. No wonder you look familiar!" Charles was going to say something polite when Naveen added, "So, my Assistant, Ronnie, is your brother. What a coincidence!"

"My brother!" exclaimed Charles faintly.

"Yes. Well, your half-brother, I suppose. Are you visiting Ronnie? He didn't mention it to me."

Charles' mind was reeling. His brother! "I.., I... no, I mean…could we sit down, please?"

Naveen looked concerned, and led him back to a chair he had just vacated, asking,

"Are you alright? Do you feel unwell? The sun must be too strong for you."

"No, no, it's just…the shock…" mumbled Charles, grappling with the idea that he might have a half-brother he had not known existed.

"Shock?" asked Naveen, looking puzzled.

"Could you tell me about … about Ronnie?" asked Charles.

Naveen looked at Charles searchingly, then understanding dawned and he asked quietly, "Did you not know that you had a half-brother?"

Charles shook his head.

"I'm so sorry. I thought you knew. Ronnie told me he had an older half-brother in England whom he had never met. Those of us who knew your father didn't know much about his early life."

Charles nodded and said slowly, "My father was a very reserved man, and firmly believed that people should only be told as much as they needed to know about his private life."

"I can understand that," said Naveen. "We tea planters tend to lead a fishbowl life. It's a tight community."

Charles said, "So, Ronnie knows about me, but I didn't even know he existed! I didn't know my father had remarried. That is, I mean… I presume…" he said uncertainly.

"Oh yes. Mr. Wentworth was married to Ronnie's mother," said Naveen, then added, "You've been talking about your father in the past tense. Does that mean…?"

"Yes, he passed away six months ago," said Charles. "I suppose Ronnie doesn't know?" he asked.

"No, no, he doesn't," said Naveen, "He would have told me. My condolences. Mr. Wentworth was highly respected by all of us who knew him."

"Thank you," said Charles. "I've brought my father's ashes to be immersed in the Brahmaputra, as he wished," he added.

"So, you are going to Assam. Where are you planning to immerse the ashes?" asked Naveen.

"I'm taking a morning flight to Guwahati the day after tomorrow," said Charles.

"Can I help in any way?" asked Naveen.

"Thank you, but the caretaker of the guest house I'm staying in is making the necessary arrangements," said Charles.

Naveen nodded, then looked at Charles searchingly and asked hesitantly, "What about Ronnie?"

Charles was still stunned by the revelation that he had a half-brother, but he knew he had to meet him. "I'd like to meet him," he said. Another thought struck him, and he asked, "Does he have siblings?"

Naveen shook his head, saying, "No, he doesn't." He paused, then continued, "Ronnie's mother lives in Guwahati. I'm flying back there this evening. If it's all right with you, I could ask him to come to Guwahati the day after tomorrow. It's just about a two-hour drive from the estate. I won't tell him anything till I meet him. I'll stay back in Guwahati, introduce you to each other, then drive back to the estate." Seeing that Charles was looking a little overwhelmed, he laughed wryly and said, "Sorry, I'm rather used to making plans and taking decisions. A big part of an estate Manager's job."

"Rather like being Captain of a ship, probably," said Charles.

"Is that what you are?" asked Naveen.

"Yes, Captain Charles Wentworth of the Royal Navy."

"Again, I'm sorry if I'm overstepping," said Naveen.

Charles shook his head and smiled faintly. "That's all right," he said. "I think I'm still in shock. Anyway, I wouldn't know where to start!" He shook his head, as if trying to clear it, and continued, "I've booked this guest house on Zoo Road for five days. I thought I'd take a drive to the estate my father worked on before he retired. I checked the map and saw that it's not very far from Guwahati. I also thought of going to the game sanctuary just outside Guwahati. Pobitora? See some rhinos if I'm lucky. Since I've come this far, I might as well see a bit of the state in which my father spent practically his whole life."

"Of course," agreed Naveen. "I can arrange your visit to Lalpani Tea Estate. The Manager there is a friend of mine." He took out his cell phone and asked, "May I have your mobile number?"

Charles said, "Sure." He called out his number, while Naveen punched in the digits. "Okay, I'll send you a message, so please save my number. It would be best if I brought Ronnie to meet you at the guest house, don't you think?"

Charles, who was still feeling lightheaded, nodded and said, "Whatever you think best."

Naveen laughed wryly again and said, "Sorry! It's force of habit, as I said."

Charles nodded saying, "It's fine. I don't think I'm in any shape to make decisions at the moment. I still feel as if someone's punched me in the gut. In fact, it's really kind of you to take such an interest in someone you met about fifteen minutes ago!"

Naveen said, "No trouble at all. I'm happy to help. As I said, I had great respect for your father and am fond of Ronnie. In fact, I think Fate arranged for us to literally bump into each other today."

He then asked for the name and address of the guest house and added them to Charles' contact details. Before putting his phone away, Naveen looked at Charles and asked hesitantly, "Would you like to see Ronnie's photo?"

Charles swallowed and nodded.

Naveen handed him the phone. "This is our club's tennis team. See if you can pick him out."

Charles stared at the photograph of four smiling men holding a trophy. His eyes immediately went to the young man who was a tanned version of his father in his younger days. Only, instead of brown hair, the young man's was black. There was no doubt at all – Ronnie was his father's son. Charles looked at the photograph for a long moment, then handed the phone back to Naveen, saying, "Thank you."

Naveen ordered another pot of tea and sat quietly with Charles, allowing him time to recover. Charles looked at Naveen and thought they must be around the same age. He asked Naveen about his family. Naveen told Charles that he was married and had two daughters, one in her last year of school and the other in college. He had been to England a few times to visit his sister who taught at Oxford. Then he talked about Charles' father and about Ronnie. He told Charles how good Ronnie was at his job, what a good sportsman he was, and how popular he was with his colleagues.

"Is he married?" asked Charles.

Naveen shook his head and said, "Not yet." He paused and said, "If you don't mind my asking, how did Mr. Wentworth pass away?"

"He suffered a series of small strokes, and then a big one which killed him," said Charles.

"Do you want me to tell Ronnie?" asked Naveen.

"Yes, thank you. I think that would be best," said Charles after a moment's thought.

"Right, then. I'll say goodbye for now," said Naveen and rose to leave. He asked Charles if he could drop him at his hotel but Charles thanked him and told him he had a hired car. They shook hands and Naveen said, "Well, it was unexpected, but a real pleasure meeting you, Captain."

"A pleasure meeting you too, Naveen. Please call me Charles," replied Charles sincerely. "Thank you very much for taking the trouble to organize my meeting with my… with Ronnie," he added.

"No trouble at all. I'm glad I could be of help," demurred Naveen. "As I said, I think we were meant to meet here today. I'll see you in Guwahati the day after tomorrow."

Charles inclined his head and said, "I look forward to that. Have a safe flight."

He watched the tall, handsome figure striding off, then sat down again, asking for another cup of tea. He tried to absorb the idea of having a half-brother, and wrinkled his brow, trying to understand why his father had kept his second marriage and the existence of a son such a secret. "You and your secrets, Dad!" thought Charles, shaking his head in exasperation.

The flight to Guwahati was smooth, and Charles was impressed with the efficient service. As the plane descended, he looked down at the river Brahmaputra meandering its way below, and thought, "Soon, I will be handing my father's ashes into your safe keeping. He wanted to come back to you." Then he thought, "Or did he want to come back to Ronnie and his mother?"

A car and driver were waiting for him at Guwahati airport. As he was driven into the city, his stomach clenched with the knowledge that he would be meeting his half-brother that evening. He wondered how Naveen would break the news of his father's death and his brother's arrival in Guwahati to Ronnie. "From what I've seen of Naveen, he'll manage to do it tactfully," thought Charles.

***

Ronnie was in the factory when his mobile rang. The noise of the machinery was very loud so he stepped out to take the call from his boss. "Good morning, Sir. I hope you enjoyed your leave in Delhi," he said.

"Yes, thanks, Ronnie. I got back to Guwahati last evening. How's everything in the factory?" asked Naveen.

"All's well, Sir." Ronnie was the Assistant Manager in charge of the factory. Though his main job was processing the freshly plucked green tea leaves into the dry leaves that were then sold in bulk, everything that happened there was his responsibility.

"Good!" said Naveen. "Ronnie, I want you to apply for three days' Casual Leave and come to Guwahati tomorrow. Sudhir will sanction it, as Acting Manager. I've already spoken to him."

"But why, Sir?" asked Ronnie, surprised. "Is my mother all right?" he asked, suddenly anxious.

"Yes, yes. Don't worry," replied Naveen reassuringly. "There's something I need you to do here. I'll explain when we meet. Leave after breakfast and let me know as soon as you reach your mother's house. That's where you'll be staying, I presume?"

"Yes, Sir," said Ronnie.

"Right, I'll see you tomorrow. I hope you're making good teas!" said Naveen.

"Yes, Sir. Pretty good!" replied Ronnie.

"Great! Keep it up. I'll see you tomorrow," said Naveen and disconnected.

Ronnie put his phone in his pocket and went back into the factory slowly. He wondered what Naveen wanted him to do in

Guwahati. If it was work related, why had he asked him to take CL? He shook his head. "No point wasting my time wondering," he thought. "I'll know soon enough." He put the matter out of his mind and got back to work.

The next day, driving to Guwahati, he wondered again why Mr. Dutta had asked him to take three days' leave and go there. Not that he was complaining! It would be a welcome break from the busy time he had been having at work. His mother was looking forward to having him home too. "As long as she hasn't lined up yet another 'eligible' girl for me to meet with a view to matrimony!" he thought. His mother was worried at his still being single.

"It's okay, Ma. No one marries young these days," he'd told her. "Besides, girls also study hard, qualify, and look for good jobs. No one is going to want to marry a tea planter and be stuck in some remote area."

His mother had lamented and asked why he didn't quit and get a job in the city. "Ma, you know I always wanted to be a tea planter. I love my job. It's interesting, and I like being outdoors. I also get to play all the sports I like."

Ronnie was an excellent sportsman. He played tennis, soccer, squash and cricket.

He suddenly realized he was driving past the estate where his father had been General Manager for five years. It had been his last posting before retirement. Ronnie felt the familiar constriction in his chest as he thought of his father. He still missed him very much. As a child, he hadn't realized that his father was much older than the fathers of his friends. He was Pa – handsome, vital, full of life. He made life interesting. Ronnie and his mother didn't live with his father. Instead, they lived in the city – Guwahati. His father visited them whenever he could, and Ronnie spent holidays with him on the tea estate. His mother never went with him. He vaguely knew why, so he never questioned her. When he was around five years old, his father had taken his mother and him to the estate for a few days. A sensitive child, Ronnie had seen the veiled hostility in the eyes of the household help and the insolence directed towards his mother behind his father's back. After all, she was from their community, so why should they treat her like a social superior? It wasn't as if she was the lady of the house, seeing that she didn't live with their Sahab permanently. She had borne it all silently, not saying a word to "Gil Sahab" as she called him, but had never gone back.

To Ronnie, the holidays spent with his father were the best times of his life. He learned to fish, play soccer, tennis, squash and cricket. His father was a great sportsman. Ronnie hoped to win as many trophies as his father when he was older. In the evening, they played board games and listened to music. His father also took him around the estate and factory, teaching him about the tea bushes and the manufacturing process. There was absolutely no doubt in Ronnie's mind that he wanted to be a tea planter like his father.

Although he was in his early teens when his father retired and left India for good, he had still cried like a baby. His mother explained that his father and she had decided this long ago. As long as he was working in Assam, he would spend time with them, but when he retired, he would go back to England.

"He has done everything for us, Ronnie. He has given me a house and enough money to live on for the rest of my life. He has given you an excellent education and is leaving money for your college fees too. He has spent all his free time with us. He has been a good father to you, Ronnie. Now, he wants to go back to his own country, and to his other son."

Ronnie bristled with jealousy. Of course, he had always known that his father had an older son from his first marriage; he had even seen photographs of him, but somehow, he had not seemed real because he had never come to India.

"Okay, I understand that Pa wants to go back to England, but why can't we go with him? We are his family!"

His mother looked at him sadly. "I can never leave Assam. This is my home – where I belong. Look at me, son, and tell me, would I ever be comfortable in a foreign country? I couldn't fit into your father's life here, how would I do so in England?" Ronnie opened his mouth to deny it, but knew it was true.

"Son," she said gently. "Pa never told his family in England about us."

"Why? Is he ashamed of us?" he cried, stung.

"No, but the circumstances were complicated, so he just let it be. His family never came here, and we never went there, so what was the point, especially when he was going back alone anyway?"

"Suppose I want to go with him?" he asked belligerently.

"No, son. Be happy with what you've had. It's time to let him go."

Ronnie stared at her aghast, feeling as if the world was collapsing around him. "But we'll be in touch with him, won't we? I could visit him when I'm older. I'll save money for the ticket."

"He'll keep in touch if he wants to. That's his choice, but there's no question of your going to see him unless he tells his family about us. Which will be difficult, after all this time."

"But he can come back and visit us," said Ronnie. His mother looked at him silently. Ronnie was unnerved and asked, "What? Why are you looking at me like that?"

"We have to let him go. He cannot be pulled two ways. Believe me, he made sacrifices for us, for you especially," said his mother.

"What sacrifices?" demanded Ronnie.

His mother hesitated, then said, "Your Pa gave you all his time, attention and love while he was here. Now, it's Charles' turn."

"But Charles must be grown up now! I need my father more! And what about you? Don't you love him? Doesn't he love you?"

His mother looked at him in silence again. Then, for the first time, she told him about the circumstances of her marriage to his father, and of his birth.

As Ronnie crossed the bridge across the Brahmaputra and turned into the city, he wondered how his father was doing. Was he in good health? He would be about eighty years old now. Since he had left, they had exchanged a few letters, but these had dwindled over the years. Ronnie had to accept the fact that his father had indeed wanted a clean break. "Perhaps it's too difficult dealing with a secret wife and son in India when he's so far away from us. It's not like he owes us anything. He gave us plenty. Looked after me till I became an adult. Gave Ma a home and an income for life." Knowing what he did now about his parents' relationship, he realized that his father had done more than his duty.

***

Charles placed the urn holding his father's ashes on the table by the window, and stood looking at it.

"What do you think about your two sons finally meeting, old man?" he thought. "Was it purely by chance that I met Naveen? Or did you somehow arrange it from wherever you are?"

Then he exclaimed aloud in frustration, "Oh, who knows what you thought? Who knows why you kept this huge secret from me? Keeping secrets was second nature to you, I suppose."

He heard the front door bell ring. The caretaker opened the door, and Charles heard Naveen's voice in the hallway. Then he and Ronnie walked into the sitting room.

Charles stood nervously by the table, staring at his brother. Naveen approached him with arm outstretched, saying, "Hello again, Charles."

Charles shook his hand warmly and said, "Hello Naveen, it's nice to see you again."

Naveen said, "Let me introduce you to Ronnie. Ronnie, this is Charles." The brothers shook hands silently. Charles nodded, not wanting to say anything trite, and Ronnie nodded back solemnly.

Naveen said, "Right. I'll take your leave now. I'm driving back to the estate. Ronnie, I'll see you back at work on Monday. Charles, it was a pleasure." He shook Charles' hand again.

Charles said sincerely, "Thank you again, Naveen."

"Thank you, Sir," said Ronnie.

Naveen smiled at them both, raised a hand in farewell and left.

Charles and Ronnie looked at each other, then Charles said, "Please, sit down." Ronnie said, "Thanks," and sat on an armchair. He stole a look at the urn. "Is that…?" he asked, unable to finish the sentence.

"Yes," said Charles quietly. "Dad's ashes are in it. He wanted me to immerse them in the Brahmaputra. I'm…I'm sorry you didn't know about his passing. Were you in touch?"

Ronnie swallowed and said, "No, not for a long time. For a couple of years or so after he left, we exchanged a few letters, but then he stopped writing, and I…I…didn't want to bother him."

"Bother him? I'm sorry, I just don't understand!" exclaimed Charles. "Why didn't he tell me about you? Why the secrecy?"

Ronnie looked away and stared at the urn. Then he mumbled, "Maybe he was ashamed."

Charles was bewildered. "Ashamed? Of what?"

Ronnie walked to the window and stood staring at the urn. He touched it gently. "My mother is from the tea garden workers' community. She was a plucker, you know. One of the workers who pluck the tea leaves from the bushes. She was seventeen years old and pretty. Pa was the Manager of the estate and she used to see him during his rounds. She had a crush on him, and probably led him on a bit. He was in his forties then. I suppose he was lonely and susceptible and she seduced him." Ronnie swallowed hard. It wasn't easy for him to talk about his mother like that, but he felt Charles deserved to know the truth. "When she became pregnant, her parents were outraged and threatened to complain to the police if he didn't marry her. She was a minor, you see, so he could've gone to jail. His career would've been over. Actually, in my mother's community, there is no stigma attached to having a child out of wedlock, but I'm sorry to say that her parents were looking at the main chance. You know, their daughter marrying the Manager. That too, an

Englishman. They thought they'd struck gold. She didn't want to force him to marry her, but he did the gentlemanly thing. She says that's when she grew up and realized that actions have consequences. He bought her a house in Guwahati, and that's where she and I lived. She cut all ties with her family because she was disgusted with their behavior. Of course, they complained to everyone saying she thought she was too good for them after marrying my father.

We didn't live with Pa on the estate but he came and spent holidays with us. It was difficult for Ma to live alone in the city with an infant, but our neighbor, a very kind lady whose late husband had been Pa's senior colleague at one time, helped her. She got a nanny for me, and someone to help Ma with the cooking and household chores. They were very inquisitive about the young, gauche girl with a baby, but Aunty Geeta, our neighbor, told them Ma was a distant relative from her native village. She very gently guided Ma into learning how to run a house and also the social graces. Over the years, Ma became more confident, and started socializing in our area, under Aunty Geeta's wing. She even started attending my parent-teacher meetings in school, of which she was terrified earlier. Aunty Geeta would attend them as my 'grandmother' before that. Pa was pleased to see Ma blossoming. I thought he'd take us to live with him then, but he didn't, and I resented that. It was only when Ma told me the truth that I realized why. I also realized that though she was devoted to him and he was very kind to her, there was no great love between them. Firstly, there was the age difference, and secondly, they had nothing in common, except me." He paused, hesitated, then said, "They had gone through a religious ceremony but their marriage was not legal, because she was a minor at the time."

"So, they weren't legally married? Is that why he didn't tell me about your mother and you?" asked Charles.

"I suppose so. And also because of who my mother was, perhaps. It was just not 'done' for an executive to marry a worker. I believe their so-called marriage was quite the scandal at the time. If Pa hadn't been so good at his job, and if my mother and I hadn't lived apart from him, he would probably have been sacked. But I didn't know any of that till Pa left. He and Ma had an understanding that he was with us as long as he was in India, but he would leave us and return to England, and you, once he retired."

Charles was silent, taking in what Ronnie had said. He could guess another reason why his father would've wanted to return to England without family ties.

Ronnie continued, "Ma told me that Pa hadn't told you or any of his family about us. Anyway, Ma could never have adjusted to life in England, and they both knew it. He legitimized me, by the way." He looked away and swallowed hard.

"Pa showed me photos of you," he continued.

Charles said, "I wish he had shown me some of **you**."

They looked at each other silently.

Then Ronnie said, "Although I was jealous of you, I fantasized about meeting you someday, you know. When I was younger."

"Why were you jealous of me?" asked Charles, surprised.

"Because he went back to you. I felt that he had chosen you over me."

Charles remained silent, then said softly, "You must have missed him very much." Ronnie turned to him and said, his voice breaking with grief, "Of course I missed him! But he wanted to return to his own country, and to you. I thought you were old enough to do without him; that I needed him more, but it was his wish!"

Charles looked at Ronnie thoughtfully, then said, "You are never too old to need a father like Gil Wentworth. Or a grandfather. My daughter Charlotte and I spent every moment we could with him. His stories about India, and life on the tea estates fascinated us. He had so much knowledge about so many things. It was a pleasure to find we had common interests. He and I both loved jazz."

"Oh yes," said Ronnie. "We used to listen to Duke Ellington, Louis Armstrong, Ella Fitzgerald. My friends thought I was crazy to listen to that kind of music rather than the latest rock, pop or Bollywood numbers." He shot a sad smile at Charles and said sincerely, "I'm glad you and Charlotte got to spend these last years with him."

"So am I," said Charles.

The caretaker brought in tea and sandwiches, which the brothers shared as they continued talking. Charles asked Ronnie how his mother had taken the news of Gil's death. "Is she all right?" he asked.

Ronnie nodded, saying, "She took it very calmly. I suppose she had let go of him when he left India all those years ago." Then he said hesitantly, "I suppose Pa didn't keep my letters, since you didn't find any among his papers. Otherwise, you would've known about me."

Charles hesitated, then said, "Actually, his will, bank details and investment papers were all in a briefcase, so we didn't need to look anywhere else. But Pat didn't mention your letters, so perhaps Dad didn't keep them. I'm sorry," he added seeing the hurt look on Ronnie's face.

"Pat?" asked Ronnie.

"Um, yes. Dad's partner," said Charles.

Ronnie wrinkled his brow and asked, "Partner? As in business partner?"

Charles hesitated, then said, "No, his live-in partner."

"Oh, had he been living with her for a long time?" asked Ronnie.

Charles replied carefully. "Him, actually. Yes, Pat and Dad were together for around fifteen years."

Ronnie was perplexed. "Him? I don't understand."

Charles said gently, "Dad was gay. It was very difficult for him while he was in India. He said the tea industry was very conservative then, especially where sexual preferences were concerned. You say his relationship with your mother was a scandal. Well, think of the bigger scandal he would have created had he come out as gay. He was very lonely, but he stuck it out till his retirement. Because of you, I suspect now. Of course, he also loved his job."

Ronnie digested that. "But… there's you… and me…"

Charles shrugged, saying, "Well, you know. It can happen…there are circumstances. I suppose the expectations from family and society led him to marry my mother, and perhaps loneliness led him to marry your mother."

Ronnie said absently, "I told you they weren't legally married."

"Well, for all intents and purposes, they were," replied Charles.

Ronnie rubbed his forehead as he stared at the urn.

"What is it?" asked Charles.

"Many things are starting to make sense now. Like why he hadn't remarried all those years after your mother left. Why he slept in the guest bedroom whenever he stayed with us… I'm…I'm sorry he couldn't be himself for all those years," said Ronnie, distressed. "Perhaps he would have returned to England much earlier if it hadn't been for me. It's my fault that he led such a lonely life."

"Hey, it's not your fault," said Charles. "Except for that one facet he kept hidden, he was himself, Ronnie. Don't feel bad. He made his own choices."

Ronnie thought about that. Then he sighed and said, "I understand now why he went back to England. I'm glad he found someone to share his life with at last. Was he happy?"

Charles nodded, saying, "Yes, he was. Very happy."

"Do you keep in touch with Pat?" asked Ronnie.

"Yes," replied Charles. "Charlotte is very fond of him. Dad left his house jointly to her and Pat. With the understanding that Pat would live there for his lifetime."

"How old is Pat?" asked Ronnie.

"He's around seventy-five now. He was a jazz musician. A saxophonist. They met at a jazz festival. He still plays, but not at events," said Charles. He took out his cell phone, flipping through it, then he handed it to Ronnie saying, "Here's a photograph of them both."

Ronnie took the phone and looked at the photograph. His father had his arm around the shoulders of a handsome man and they were both smiling happily into the camera. His father didn't look much older than he had the last time Ronnie had seen him – before he'd left Assam.

"That was taken on Dad's 75th birthday," said Charles.

"He looks fit," said Ronnie.

"Yes, he was. The strokes only started happening a year ago," explained Charles. Ronnie looked at the photograph again, then handed the phone back to Charles. "Would you like me to send it to you?" asked Charles.

"Yes, please. And any other photos you have of Pa," said Ronnie.

"Sure. Call out your cell phone number," said Charles. As Ronnie called out the digits, Charles punched them in. 'So, is your name Ronnie or Ronald Wentworth?" he asked.

"Actually, it's Ronojoy James Wentworth," clarified Ronnie.

"Hey, James is my middle name too!" exclaimed Charles. "It was our grandfather's name," he explained.

"Really?" asked Ronnie, feeling touched and very pleased. "It never occurred to me to ask Pa, actually. But I'm honored to bear our grandfather's name. What was he like?" he asked.

"Umm, just let me send you the photographs, and then I'll tell you about Gramps," said Charles. "What does Ronojoy mean?" he asked.

"It means 'victorious in battle,'" explained Ronnie.

"Oh, nice," commented Charles.

They sat and talked more easily, no more secrets between them. Ronnie listened with interest as Charles told him about their family. Then Ronnie invited Charles to spend a couple of days with him on the tea estate.

"You could drive down with me, and we could stop at Lalpani Tea Estate on the way," he suggested.

"I'd like that very much, thanks," said Charles.

When the caretaker came in to switch on the lights and ask Charles what he would like to have for dinner, Charles asked Ronnie to join him. They had dinner, and chatted till about 10 o'clock.

Then Ronnie said, "I must leave now. Ma will start worrying otherwise." A thought struck him and he mused aloud. "I wonder if Ma knew about Pa being gay. She did mention something about his having made sacrifices…"

"Well, she may have guessed. Or he may have even told her," said Charles. "Perhaps that's why she was so adamant about my letting him go," mused Ronnie. "She wanted him to have his own life in England. And he more than deserved that."

Ronnie realized that he could at last accept his father's decision without feeling let down and abandoned as he'd done for so long.

"I'm so glad he found Pat," he said again.

He held out his hand and said, "Thank you for dinner Charles, and for clearing up some things that have worried me for so long."

Charles shook his hand without commenting.

"I can't believe I've actually met my elder brother!" exclaimed Ronnie. "Thank you for…for acknowledging me," he added.

Charles felt a lump in his throat, and murmured, "Of course," grasping Ronnie's hand hard with both of his.

"I'm sorry if it was a shock, you know, finding out you had a half-brother," said Ronnie awkwardly.

Charles cleared his throat and said, "Yes, it was rather a shock when Naveen told me about you. But I'm glad." He paused, then added, "Listen, I realize you're entitled to some of Dad's estate…"

But Ronnie cut him short saying, "No, no. He gave me enough. The rest is yours." Charles was silent, thinking that perhaps this hadn't been the right time to bring up the topic.

"Well, now I'm here to fulfil Dad's last wish," he said quietly, "and I have a brother to help me."

"You want me to immerse his ashes with you?" asked Ronnie.

"Of course!" replied Charles. "It's your right."

Ronnie shook Charles hand again, saying sincerely, "Thank you." He dashed tears out of his eyes.

Trying to lighten the mood, Charles said teasingly, "It's a little uncanny seeing someone who looks so much like Dad did in his younger days."

"And a little uncanny seeing someone who looks so much like he did when I was a child!" returned Ronnie.

"Yes," laughed Charles. They looked at their reflection in the mirror hanging on one wall. "Good God! We're the same height and build!" exclaimed Charles.

"That makes it easy for you to wear my clothes tomorrow," said Ronnie. When Charles looked at him enquiringly, he explained. "We usually wear white clothes to do this kind of ceremony."

"Ceremony?" asked Charles. "We've had a funeral service for him already, so I thought we were just going to immerse the ashes!"

"We do that after some rituals," said Ronnie "I would like to do it properly for Pa, if you don't mind."

"No, no, of course I don't mind," exclaimed Charles, "We'll scatter his ashes with all due respect. Let's ask the caretaker what arrangements he's made."

It turned out that the caretaker had already asked a priest to be at the riverside before the auspicious time, which was 11 AM. "I'll take you there, Sir," he told Charles. "I'll get all the necessary items, like flowers, incense sticks, a coconut etc. The priest has given me a list."

"Thank you, Hiren," said Charles. "Please meet me before you go to buy the items, so that I can give you the money for them."

Hiren said, "Sure, Sir," and left the room.

"I'll bring the clothes at around 10 AM tomorrow, and we can go to the riverside together. Is that okay?" asked Ronnie.

"That sounds fine," said Charles. Then a thought struck him and he asked, "Would your mother like to join us?"

Ronnie said, "I'll ask her. Afterwards, perhaps you'd like to come and have lunch with us."

"I would love that," said Charles.

The next day, Charles wore the white "churidar" and "kurta" that Ronnie had lent him, and the two brothers went down to the banks of the Brahmaputra along with Hiren. Ronnie's mother had decided not to join them, but had seconded Ronnie's invitation to Charles to join Ronnie and her for lunch at their place.

The rituals and chants, though alien to Charles, made him feel like his father was being sent off on his last journey with proper respect. He glanced at Ronnie's solemn face, and was glad that his brother had got to do this for their father and bid him goodbye.

Charles watched the ashes spread on the water and get carried away by the waves. "Well, Dad, your last wish has been fulfilled," he said silently, then added, "Or did you actually have two wishes?"

He glanced at the profile so like his father's, and his own, and thought how his chance encounter with Naveen had brought all this about. Fate, or Gil Wentworth?

Incognito

Fate decrees that to hide in plain sight,

one has to go incognito.

Abdul grimaced as he looked in the mirror and adjusted his peaked cap. He thought the chauffer's uniform looked smart enough without the cap, but the Visiting Agent – his boss – thought otherwise. Thank goodness he only had to wear it when he was driving important visitors around!

He had his breakfast, then walked from his quarters to the Visiting Agent's bungalow through the small side gate that all the drivers and household staff used. He was one of three drivers assigned to the Visiting Agent, who was the Company's top executive on the tea estates. The bungalow was impressive – an old colonial two-storied structure with massive rooms and high ceilings.

The previous evening, Abdul had been told which car he was to take to the airport that morning, so he had filled the fuel tank and checked the vehicle up thoroughly. An important visitor was arriving with his wife and staying for two days.

"Babul will go with you to handle the luggage," said Mr. Choudhury, who looked after all the logistics regarding the Visiting Agent's company guests. "I've given him the placard with the visitors' names, which he'll hold up while he waits for them to come out of the airport. He'll give you a call as soon as they do, so that you can drive to the pick-up area immediately. Understood, Abdul?"

"Yes Sir," replied Abdul respectfully, thinking, "I've done this at least a hundred times before!"

Now, as he entered the garage, he saw Babul waiting near the car.

"Good morning, Abdul," he called out.

Abdul returned his greeting, picked up the car key from the holder and unlocked the doors. He slid into the driver's seat and started the car. Babul sat on the passenger seat, fastening his seat belt. Abdul liked Babul because he didn't chatter unnecessarily.

The drive to the airport took an hour, which passed quickly as they listened to music. It was a small airport with outdoor parking. Abdul parked under a tree so that the car seats wouldn't get hot while they waited. Babul got off and taking his placard, walked to the Arrivals gate. Abdul took off his cap, lit a cigarette and puffed comfortably while he waited for Babul's call, which came after half an hour. Donning his cap again, Abdul drove to the pick-up area and stopped in front of Babul and the visitors. He pulled the lever that unlocked the trunk, so that Babul could place the luggage inside. Then he got out and opened both the back doors. The gentleman and lady both thanked him but the lady was busy rooting around in her handbag for her sunglasses, so she didn't look at him. For the very first time, Abdul was thankful for his chauffer's peaked cap. Heart thudding, he got into the driver's seat and started the car. During the drive, he glanced at her reflection in the rear-view mirror from time to time. She was still very beautiful.

After dropping the visitors at the bungalow, Abdul cleaned the car, locked it and walked home. He threw himself on the bed, lit a cigarette, and let his mind drift back twenty-five years.

***

His name was Kasim and he lived in his family's three-storied house in Park Circus, Calcutta with his father. His mother had died when he was twelve. It was a loss he hadn't got over, though his father had done his best to be both parents to him.

His father owned a rubber factory in the outskirts of the city, in which he manufactured soles for shoes and straps for slippers, which he supplied to big shoe companies. The business had been built by Kasim's grandfather but after his death, his brothers had tried to claim a share of it. Fortunately, Kasim's father, Faisal, had hired a good lawyer who ensured that he had inherited the whole business. Obviously, after that, Faisal had been estranged from his uncles, but he didn't consider it much of a loss.

Faisal was honest and hardworking. He had a reputation for keeping his word and delivering on his promises. The business flourished but the hard work and undercutting by his rivals took their toll on Faisal's health. When he suddenly died of a heart attack at fifty, Kasim inherited the business, the house, and all his father's money.

A rich man at nineteen! Since Kasim's father had been estranged from his relatives, and his mother's family had cut off all relations with her when she had eloped with his father, there was no family member to guide him about handling his inheritance.

Kasim dropped out of college, bought swanky cars and smoked the best cigarettes, though he didn't touch alcohol, as it was against his religion. He also bought a Jeep which had been modified for rally driving, and started participating in car rallies.

Of course, he attracted a lot of sycophants in the guise of friends, and beautiful girls threw themselves at him, but he had eyes only for his childhood friend, Saira. They had loved each other since their early teens and always knew they'd get married one day. But her father had wanted him to make something of himself first.

"You should at least graduate, and then start looking after the business, instead of driving around in fancy cars. Only then will

I agree to Saira marrying you. I don't want her to marry a rich man's spoilt son."

Kasim didn't understand that kind of thinking. "Why should I waste my time on studies when I don't have to?" he asked Saira. "We'll live in our family home and I'll learn the business. How hard can it be?" he asked with the arrogance of youth.

Calcutta in the early 1970s was still famous for its night clubs and restaurants such as Moulin Rouge, Blue Fox, Trinca's and Mocambo, all located along Park Street, which was the most "happening" place to spend nights out partying and dancing to the music of the talented singers and live bands who performed in those restaurants. On any given night, Kasim would be at one or the other with his entourage. He also frequented the fabled Firpo's – erstwhile haunt of the city's elite – doomed to close a few years later.

Saira's father refused to allow her out with him at night, even in a crowd of friends.

"I don't like those so-called 'friends' of his," he commented. "They're only with him for his money. I wonder if they ever open their own wallets or purses."

Saira knew he was right. In fact, she tried to open Kasim's eyes about these friends but he just brushed away her concerns.

One of his new "friends" introduced him to a bookie at the race course. Kasim started winning large sums of money, and before he knew it, gambling on horses had become an addiction. Soon, he started losing money.

Saira was concerned and begged him to stop gambling, saying, "We're getting married in a few years' time. We'll start a family. You can't gamble away your children's inheritance; the inheritance your father and your grandfather before him built with such hard work and dedication. Please, please, Kasim. Just stop now before it's too late!"

Saira's father gave him an ultimatum. "You either stop this nonsense or forget my daughter!" he said firmly, refusing to let him meet Saira till he had come to his senses.

But Kasim kept thinking he'd win back his money, and threw good money after bad. His schoolfriend, Tuhin, tried to make him stop, but his entreaties fell on deaf ears, unfortunately. Kasim sold his business and his cars, but still owed money to the bookie and to others. When he had to sell his house as well, Tuhin, whose family owned majority shares in a tea company, decided to pack him off to one of the company's remote estates in Assam.

"I wish I had listened to you!" exclaimed Kasim.

"Too late now," said Tuhin grimly. "Before you get thrown in jail by your creditors, you had better disappear. No one will find you in that remote part of Assam. You had better change your name, though, just in case. What name would you like to use, by the way?"

Kasim rubbed his forehead tiredly and said, "I'll use my grandfather's name – Abdul."

Kasim looked so miserable and defeated that Tuhin felt bad for him. "Look, my dad has agreed to give you a job in one of our estates, but you'll have to work as a driver and live in one of the staff quarters. I'm sorry my friend, but that's the only job he can offer you, and it's also the only way you can remain incognito. Okay?"

Kasim nodded. He was too tired and miserable to care, but he thought of Saira. "What'll I tell Saira?" he asked Tuhin. "Her father will never allow her to marry me now. But she might run away with me."

Tuhin had never met Saira, but he looked at Kasim straight and asked, "Do you think it's fair to ask her to give up everything and live a fugitive's life with you?"

Kasim realized that he had forfeited every right to ask Saira to marry him. That night, he wept bitter tears. He wanted to write her a letter apologizing and explaining why he had to disappear. He wrote at least five drafts but tore them all up. What was the use? Better to make a clean break and let her get on with her life. The thought of her married to someone else tore at his guts but he gritted his teeth. He had brought it all on himself. Now the fever that had led him to gamble his whole fortune away seemed like some nightmare that had happened long ago to someone else. He shook his head as if to clear it. If only... he wiped his tears and tried to sleep.

He went over the list of his debts with Tuhin, who said he would pay each of his debtors a quarter of what was owed to him. "I'll get someone I trust to deliver the money to them as a gesture of good faith. He'll say he's your representative, and that you'll be paying your debts slowly. You can send me a bit of your salary every month and I'll pay one of them. When all your debts are paid, you can return what you owe me. Till then, you'll have to stay out of sight, otherwise they'll hound you for the whole amount, or go to the police."

Kasim nodded miserably. "I will. Reporters are also hounding me. I can't believe the rubbish they're writing about me now! I don't know what I would've done without you. Thanks, Tuhin."

Tuhin patted his shoulder consolingly. "Look, I hope you can come back to Calcutta again someday."

Kasim shook his head. "What should I come back for? I've lost everything!" "Everything!" he repeated softly, biting his lip as he thought of Saira. "None of my so-called friends want to know me. They run in the other direction when they see me. You are my only friend. Thanks for doing so much for me. I promise, I won't let you down." Tuhin patted his shoulder again.

When Tuhin thought of those "fair weather friends" who had latched on to Kasim like leeches when the going was good, he felt the fury rise in him. He looked at the crestfallen young man and wished he could do more for him.

However, his father had said, "Help him, yes, Tuhin. But don't coddle him. He has to bear the consequences of his actions. That's the only way he'll become a responsible man."

"But Dad, why a driver? Can't he work as an Assistant Manager? Or even a clerk in the office?"

Tuhin's father had looked at him squarely. "I thought he wanted to change his name from Kasim to Abdul and remain incognito. How would he apply for an Assistant Manager's post without proper papers? His application would go to the HR department and he'd have to appear for an interview if called. Besides, he doesn't have the qualifications. As for clerical staff applications, they all come to the estate from the local Employment Exchange. As Chairman of the company, the only job I can offer him without consulting the Board or HR is a driver's. One thing he does well is drive, thanks to those fancy cars he owned, and thanks to his rally driving."

He looked at his son and said more gently, "I'm proud of you, son. You are kind and compassionate. But don't let those qualities make you weak, or cloud your judgment. You're giving him a job, a place to stay, and also helping to pay off his debts. It'll take time, and that might be the making of him. I've sent instructions to the Manager of the estate saying Kasim, I mean Abdul, is the son of an old and valued family retainer, so he should be treated well. That'll be enough to ensure his wellbeing."

"Thanks, Dad," said Tuhin affectionately.

So Kasim had arrived at the tea estate in due course and met the Head Clerk at the office. He was given his appointment letter and the terms and conditions of his job. He hadn't asked Tuhin what his salary would be, but realized that he was being paid a very good sum, taking into account the fact that his accommodation and medical care were free. He would be able to send a tidy sum to Tuhin by Money Order every month.

After his palatial family home in Calcutta, the driver's quarters were really small and sparsely furnished. "Beggars can't be choosers!" he told himself firmly. "Be happy you have a roof over your head."

He was put on hospital duty, which meant he had to drive the ambulance. The hours were regular but he sometimes had to report for emergencies. Over the months, he got used to his new life. He kept to himself as he didn't want to answer a lot of questions. He got used to being called Abdul, and after a while, almost forgot that wasn't his real name. His rally driving over rough terrain came in useful now, as he had to drive the ambulance over slippery boulders lining the river bed while crossing the river between the estate and the central hospital where serious patients had to be taken. The river had no bridge across it, and sometimes flash floods caused by rain in the hills raised the water level and made driving across the river a hazardous exercise. He found that he could keep calm and drive across even when the waters were high and the current quite strong.

He also found that he was quite useful in a medical emergency because he could keep a cool head and wasn't squeamish about seeing injuries or blood. The doctor advised him to do a course in first aid, so that he would be qualified to help the paramedics as first responders. He said he wasn't a graduate, but the doctor said that didn't matter, as long as he had finished high school. Abdul replied that he had lost his school leaving certificate, but the doctor said he would recommend Abdul for the course all the same.

After Abdul had been on the estate for ten years, the Manager's driver retired and Abdul was chosen to replace him. He hadn't expected a promotion so soon, but was happy when he realized that he would get a higher grade which came with better living quarters and a higher salary. He would also have the prestige of being the Manager's driver. The doctor and medical staff were sorry to lose him, but they knew it was a well-deserved promotion.

In the last ten years, Abdul hadn't met Tuhin's father on any of his visits to the estate, although he had seen him from afar on one or two occasions. But now, as the Manager's driver, he had to sometimes drive him around the estate when he visited.

When they met the first time, the Chairman asked Abdul cordially, "How are you, Abdul? I hope you have settled down well and are enjoying your work."

"Yes, Sir, thank you," Abdul had replied sincerely.

During subsequent visits, he would get a nod and smile in greeting, and a "Thank you," at the end of the visit. Even that much recognition coming from the Chairman was enough to send Abdul's stock rising. His new boss asked him how he knew the Chairman, so Abdul replied saying his father had worked in the Chairman's household.

When Abdul's boss realized that he could read and write English, he was given more and more responsibilities over and above his duties as a driver. Abdul never spoke in English or let on that he could understand it. That would have given rise to too many questions.

"Where did you learn to read and write English?" his boss asked.

"I just learned it over the years, Sir," replied Abdul vaguely. He made it a point to make a few spelling mistakes and keep the language very rudimentary.

One day his boss asked him why he wasn't married. Immediately, Saira's sweet face filled his mind and he winced, but said levelly, "I'm very happy on my own, Sir. I don't think I'm the marrying kind."

"Well, selfishly, I'm glad, because you don't have anything to distract you from your work," said his boss.

Abdul smiled politely, saying, "Yes, Sir."

One early morning that summer, while the Manager was in his office and his wife was out on her walk, their 10-year-old son, Ishaan, was cycling around the lawn, when he suddenly lost control and fell on the hedge. Trying to save himself, he instinctively grabbed at the hedge, but his hand went through a bare patch grabbing the barbed wire fence behind it, and a spike entered his palm. Abdul was washing the car when he heard the screams, and ran in their direction. He saw the gardeners standing and looking at the boy helplessly. Abdul took charge and sent one of them to fetch the first-aid kit he always kept in the car, and another on his bicycle to the factory to fetch a wire-cutter. He calmed the boy down, then swiftly and efficiently cut the wires, maneuvered the spike out of the palm, cleaned and dressed the wound, then drove Ishaan to the hospital. Fortunately, they met the boy's mother on the way, so he stopped and picked her up, explaining what had happened.

At the hospital, the doctor put in two stitches and commended Abdul on his quick action. From then onwards, throughout the summer holidays, Ishaan became his shadow. Abdul liked the boy, who was intelligent and polite. When his parents admonished Ishaan for disturbing Abdul, the latter said he didn't mind at all. Looking at the boy, Abdul sometimes wondered what his and Saira's children would've been like. But those kinds of thoughts were painful so he deliberately brought his mind back to the present. Ishaan asked him questions about the car and seemed to grasp whatever Abdul told him. Abdul himself read every car manual meticulously, so he knew what he was talking about.

When the Manager was transferred on promotion to another estate, the whole family was sad to leave their home of five years, their household staff, and most of all, Abdul. He was sorry to see them go too. His boss had always been kind, as had been his wife, and he had become really fond of Ishaan.

The new Manager was a decent man, and treated Abdul with respect. His wife was a kind person too. They had two sons, both in college. The times had changed in this remote area of Assam in the last few years. The local young men were dissatisfied with their lives and felt ignored by the state government.

Abdul's boss told his wife, "Well, just look at how backward this area is. There aren't any development projects, no bridges over the rivers, no job opportunities. I can't really blame them."

However, it was the tea planters who became the targets of the militant group when it was formed. A special security force had to be raised for their protection. Abdul's boss had to have five security personnel with him at all times. They sat in the back of the open Gypsy, weapons held at the ready. It was rather unnerving, and sometimes Abdul was afraid the weapons might go off if the vehicle bumped too hard on the rough, unpaved roads. He was reassured when he was told that the safety catch was always on.

One evening, Abdul was driving his boss home across the river after a Managers' meeting at the club. The water level was a little higher than normal and the current was strong, so he had to drive carefully. The current could force the vehicle to move off course, and get swept away. That could be dangerous and even fatal.

Suddenly, he heard a strange "whooshing" sound and then a series of "thunks," as if hail stones were hitting the car. He heard one of the security guards shout "Duck!" while forcing his boss' head down. Then they opened fire.

"Drive!" one of them shouted at him. Abdul, adrenaline pumping, let the rally driver in him take over. How he drove the damaged vehicle across the river and safely home, he had no idea! Miraculously, though everyone was shaken, and even bruised from the bumpy ride, no one had been shot. The Gypsy, however, was very badly damaged.

Abdul's boss was full of praise for him, as were the guards. They all thanked him for saving their lives. Abdul said he was just glad the vehicle hadn't packed up in the middle of the river.

"Where did you learn to drive like that?" his boss asked.

"Years of practice driving the ambulance across the river, and then this Gypsy, Sir," he replied vaguely.

He was embarrassed by all the attention from everyone on the estate, but appreciated the letter of commendation from the Chairman of the company, Tuhin's father. What he treasured most were the heartfelt "thank you" from his boss' wife, and a letter from their two sons. He also appreciated the fact that he was not offered any monetary "reward" because that would have demeaned the whole episode for him. What had scared him was the reporter from a national newspaper who had wanted to interview him. He didn't want his picture in the paper in case someone recognized him, so he was nowhere to be found the day the reporter came to the estate. The Manager narrated the events to the reporter whose editor then gave the report one column on an inside page. Abdul smiled wryly when he saw that. He had panicked for nothing.

Life went on, but after five years, when his old boss became the Visiting Agent, he had Abdul transferred to his establishment. Ishaan, now fifteen, was very glad to see his old friend and "savior" whenever he came home on holiday from his boarding school. Abdul always drove Ishaan's mother or father to the airport to pick him up or see him off. He was very fond of Ishaan and knew that Ishaan was fond of him too, because he always hung around him and brought him a gift every time he came home. Abdul kept them all carefully in a box. He sometimes took them out to admire, and smile over, because some of them were wildly inappropriate – such as the cologne.

"How can I use cologne, or wear sunglasses to work?" he had protested.

"Hey, you are a smart, good-looking man. Use them on your days off at least," Ishaan had replied, grinning.

Abdul did dab on some on his days off, and wore the sunglasses too. The Swiss knife was very useful. He kept it with him at all times.

There were occasions when he drove his boss and his wife to the club or to parties that he was reminded of his heydays in Calcutta. But they now seemed very distant. He had paid off most of his debts, but still owed Tuhin money. When mobile phones had come into the market, his boss had bought him one, saying jokingly, "Now, I can disturb you whenever I want!"

Abdul had respectfully asked the Chairman for Tuhin's number when he'd had the chance. The Chairman had handed him a folded piece of paper discreetly after a few minutes. Since then, he and Tuhin had kept in touch over the phone. Tuhin had asked him again if he wanted to return to Calcutta once all his debts were paid, but Abdul knew that Kasim was dead and gone, and so was the old life in Calcutta, now called "Kolkata." He had never asked Tuhin to find out about Saira. Better to forget her. He just hoped she had forgotten him, and was happy.

***

A small sound broke Abdul's reverie, bringing him back to the present. He knew now that Saira had married well. He tried to remember what he'd been told about her husband by Mr. Choudhury. Not much, but he was obviously someone important, to be treated as a VIP and entertained by the company's Visiting Agent. Saira was well groomed and well dressed. She and her husband seemed to be on good terms judging from their conversation on the drive from the airport. They laughed together and he was attentive towards her. Abdul was glad. Somehow, after seeing her, he felt better. All these years, he had never been able to marry. His guilt had held him back initially, but soon he had grown used to being on his own and was quite content with his books, music, and his own company.

The next day, Abdul reported for duty, feeling quite apprehensive that Saira might recognize him. He was asked to park the car in the porch and wait. He did so, and saw Saira sitting on the verandah, chatting with the Visiting Agent's wife. As he parked the car, alighted and shut the door, she glanced at him casually, but looked away almost immediately. Once again, Abdul was glad of the peaked cap. He was sure she hadn't recognized him. He had changed in the last twenty-five years, thanks to the exercise regime he still followed religiously. His face had become leaner and his body had become more muscular. Anyway, she would never expect to see him in this remote tea estate.

The men came out of the bungalow, said their goodbyes to the ladies and got into the car. Abdul greeted them and waited for instructions.

"Abdul, we're visiting Bokul Tea Estate today. Drive us straight to the Manager's office there, please," said his boss.

"Yes, Sir," said Abdul as he started the car.

Throughout the half hour's drive, Abdul glanced at Saira's husband in the rear-view mirror. His boss addressed him as Abid. He was handsome and distinguished looking, and had a pleasant voice. He was well dressed too. Abdul thought he looked like a nice person. He wondered if he and Saira had children. He found he could think of Saira as Abid's wife and the mother of his children without wincing or feeling like throwing up. He realized that he had needed to see her again in order to get closure and was thankful that Fate had arranged it. Perhaps seeing her alone would not have been the same but seeing her with Abid was probably the best thing that could have happened.

When they reached the Bokul Tea Estate office, the two men got out of the car, and Abid thanked Abdul with a smile. "Impeccable manners too!" thought Abdul. He liked the man and was thankful that Saira had married him.

He used a duster to clean the car, then went to the adjoining factory canteen to drink a cup of tea. As the VA's driver, he was treated with respect and offered snacks to go with the tea. He accepted the mark of favor graciously, and opened the newspaper he was carrying. Although he tried to read it, his mind kept going back to the past, and the times he'd spent with Saira.

***

The first time he realized how lovely his childhood friend had grown was when he was fifteen and she was thirteen.

His friend, Faiz, commented on it, saying, "Kasim, your friend Saira has grown into a beauty!"

Kasim frowned at him and glanced at Saira, who was talking and laughing with her friend, Shahnaaz. For the first time, he really **looked** at her instead of just seeing her.

He'd felt a queer sensation in the general area of his heart, and glowered at Faiz, saying, "Stop staring at her and thinking bad thoughts!"

Faiz vigorously denied thinking "bad thoughts" and hastily changed the subject.

After that, Kasim started visiting Saira's home quite frequently, on one pretext or another. Fortunately, his father and Saira's were both avid readers and exchanged books regularly, usually using Kasim as the courier. Earlier, he had chafed at doing this errand but now he wished both men read faster! Craftily, he ensured that he went to Saira's place on a Wednesday evening when she and her mother were sure to be listening to the top Hindi film hits on the radio. He would then show a keen interest in the songs, and sit with them. While mother and daughter chatted with each other, he would look at Saira's face wonderingly. When had that imp of a girl become this entrancing beauty? She sometimes glanced at him questioningly but he just smiled.

On one occasion, not wanting to outstay his welcome, he got up to leave during a commercial break, but Saira's mother asked innocently, "Don't you want to wait till the end to hear the top song of the week?"

He hastily agreed and sat down again. After that, it had become the accepted thing for him to listen to the program with them.

Once, Saira's father saw him and remarked in surprise, "I didn't know you were such a fan of Hindi film songs, Kasim."

Squirming in embarrassment, Kasim said, "I...I like this program, actually." Saira's father shot him a sardonic look before leaving the room. Poor Kasim sat through the rest of the program with burning ears. He decided to make an excuse about the next Wednesday before leaving, but Saira smiled at him sweetly and said, "Bye Kasim. See you next Wednesday. We'll bet and see which song is Number 1, okay?"

He nodded dumbly, somehow mumbled "Thank you. Goodbye," to her and her mother, and stumbled home.

Remembering how Faiz had noticed Saira's newly blooming beauty, he thought hard and long about his feelings for her. When he thought of other boys looking at her, he felt murderous. He concluded that he must be in love with her. The problem was he had no idea about her feelings for him. Little did he know that all he had to do was ask Shahnaaz! The longsuffering girl had to listen to Saira's constant paeans about his looks, smile, and voice. Kasim didn't realize that while he thought her eyes were glued to the radio, she was actually looking at his reflection in the small, ornate mirror above it!

After a great deal of ruminating, Kasim decided to write to her about his feelings. He tried to keep it casual, then thought that might be disrespectful. He decided it would be best to just be honest, so he wrote from his heart. The next Wednesday, heart thumping, he silently handed her the letter when her mother left the room to get a cold drink and some snacks for him. She raised her eyebrows enquiringly but he gestured that she should hide it away. She folded the letter and put it into her pocket. Little did he realize how her heart was thumping!

The next day, as he was walking to school, Shahnaaz ran up to him and handed him a letter, then ran back to Saira, who gave him a shy glance before quickly walking on with Shahnaaz. With shaking hands, Kasim hastily stuffed the letter into his satchel just as Faiz ran up to him and thumped him on the back.

"That was the beginning of our sweet and rather innocent romance," thought Kasim, "which would have culminated in marriage if I hadn't ruined everything with my madness."

He imagined life with Saira in his family home. He would go to work every morning, and look forward to coming home to her at the end of each day. What heaven that would have been!

"Well, she's married to a good man. She's happy, as she deserves to be. Now, I can let her go." He wondered if she ever thought about him. "Probably hates my guts! And who could blame her!" he thought morosely.

The next morning, he reported for duty and was told he was to drive the visitors to the airport. Babul would be going with him to see to their luggage. Again, Abdul was thankful for the peaked cap. He opened the trunk for Babul to load the luggage, then opened the rear doors for Saira and her husband. Both got in and thanked him, but Saira's eyes were on her phone, as she was busy texting. He couldn't help glancing at her from time to time in the rear-view mirror, thinking regretfully that this might be the last time he'd see her. He wanted to etch her face in his memory.

They reached the airport, and Abdul stopped at the drop-off point. He quickly unlocked the trunk for Babul to take the suitcases out, then opened the door on Saira's side. As she got off, she looked him full in the face and straight into his eyes. Shocked, he realized that she must have recognized him either the day she and Abid had arrived, or from the time she had glanced at him while he waited on the porch. Mesmerized, he just stared at her, till he heard Abid's voice saying her name. She turned towards her husband, who handed her an envelope containing money, inclining his head towards Abdul. Taking it from him, she slipped a folded piece of paper in it and handed it to Abdul, saying, "Thank you." Her fingers touched his for a second, and looking into her eyes, he saw a mixture of emotions reflected in them. Then she turned and walked away with her husband.

Abdul stood looking at them till he heard Babul say, "Hey, let's get out of here before we are chased away."

Abdul lifted the flap of the envelope and saw a small, folded piece of paper lying on top of two five-hundred-rupee notes. Unfolding the piece of paper, he read the five words scrawled in bold letters. Then he folded it and placed it back in the envelope and stuffed it into his pocket. Taking off the peaked cap and throwing it on the back seat, he drove away. He switched on the music and drummed his fingers on the steering wheel.

Babul glanced at him and smiled, saying, "You seem to be in a good mood, Abdul."

"I am, Babul, I am!" said Abdul, smiling back.

"Take care and be happy." Five simple, even banal words, but to Abdul, they conveyed the most important message in the world – that he was forgiven.

Just An Old Tea Chest

Who knows what treasures Fate has

hidden in an old box?

Michael Fletcher walked around the small, attractively laid out garden center, admiring the flowering plants, lush ferns and exotic orchids. He was looking for a couple of sturdy potted plants to place around his newly refurbished house. The owner of the garden center, Paul Simmons, had already picked out four which he said did not need too much looking after. After some deliberation, Michael picked up a Peace Lily and a red flower, quite like a lily, but which Paul identified as an anthurium.

Michael laughed, saying, "I like plants but don't really know much about them, as you can see."

Paul said, "We all have our areas of expertise, Michael. I wouldn't be able to identify a single quote from Shakespeare's plays!"

Michael said mischievously, "I could lend you my Complete Works of Shakespeare."

Paul recoiled in mock horror saying, "Please, Professor, spare me the torture!"

Paul helped Michael load the potted plants into the back of Michael's small truck, giving him some last-minute advice.

Struck by a thought, he said, "I've got some new garden ornaments – statues and stuff – lying in the shed at the back. I haven't had the time to display them yet. Would you like to take a look?"

Michael said, "Sure, lead the way," and followed Paul to the shed.

He looked around with interest at the frogs in various poses, flamingos, herons, mermaids and vaguely oriental looking figures, till his eyes alighted on a stone figure. It was a potbellied man with an elephant's head. The eyes were the most friendly and benign he had ever seen on a statue. The figure had four arms, each holding some kind of implement or weapon, and a mouse at his feet. Intrigued, he moved closer to the statue – which was around two feet high – and stood staring at it.

Paul walked up to him and said, "That's a statue of the Indian god, Ganesh. The Hindu god, I should've said. He is believed to be the remover of obstacles. There's a legend about how he got an elephant's head, but I don't really know that story."

"I'll take it," said Michael firmly.

"Right, let's see what we can pack it in," said Paul, looking around the shed. Michael looked around too, and spied a lidless wooden box, which looked like it had seen better days.

"There's a box," he said, pointing.

Paul said, "Oh, that old tea chest. It's been lying there since my parents' stuff arrived here from England. I think Mum's books came in that."

Michael walked up to the box and stood looking at it. For some reason, his eyes were drawn to the lettering on its sides. "DUBBORI T.E." was written in large, bold letters on one side along with a logo, while what looked like an address in India and the year "1991" were stenciled on another.

"Why did you call it a tea chest?" he asked Paul.

"Well, that's what it is. It originally carried tea leaves from India to England. My dad got the empty box from a friend."

Michael looked at the lettering again and asked, "What does DUBBORI T.E. mean?"

Paul shrugged, saying, "No idea. I think the statue will fit in it, though. Shall we see?"

Michael followed Paul back to the statue and watched as Paul wrapped it with protective material. He handed Paul pieces of tape to seal the packing, saying, "Quite appropriate, really, isn't it?"

Paul asked, "What?" as he lined the box with old newspapers.

Michael picked up the statue, which was quite heavy, and placed it carefully in the box, "The statue of an Indian god being packed in a box also originally from India."

Paul smiled and nodded, saying, "Yes, you're right. Quite a coincidence, really."

The two men then lifted the box and carried it to the truck.

"Have you ever been to India?" Michael asked Paul.

Paul shook his head, and asked, "You?"

Michael said, "Me neither, but it's on my wish list. Even more so now that I have this statue and this box. I'd like to know more about both."

Paul said, "Well, I'm sure there'll be plenty about Ganesh on the internet, but I'm not too sure about the tea chest. Let me talk to Dad and see if he can tell you anything."

"Thanks, that would be great, Paul," said Michael.

Paul nodded and said, "I'm not sure how much he knows, though."

Michael said, "That's all right. I'd be grateful for whatever information he has."

"How are you going to offload it when you get home?" asked Paul.

"My neighbor's a helpful chap. I'll give him a shout," replied Michael.

"Okay, I'll just check the invoice and see the price of the statue," said Paul.

After paying what he thought was a very reasonable price for the statue, and getting the box thrown in for free, Michael took his leave.

Once he got home, he unloaded his truck with the help of his neighbor, Guy, and took the potted plants and the tea chest into the small foyer. Guy helped him to lift the statue out of the box and watched as he unwrapped it. "That's an interesting character!" he exclaimed.

"He's called Ganesh," said Michael, "and he's a Hindu god from India."

Guy read the lettering on the box and asked, "Oh, so this is the box he came in from India?"

Michael shook his head, saying, "No, this box was packed with tea which travelled from India to England, originally."

Guy nodded without much interest and said, "Do you want me to help place him somewhere?" Michael thanked him and said he'd manage.

"Right, if we're done, I'll just toddle home then," said Guy, who was rather prone to using such terms, being an avid reader of P.G. Wodehouse's books.

Michael thanked him and turned back to the statue.

He decided to keep Ganesh in the house instead of out in the garden. He placed the statue in one corner of the drawing room and arranged the two flowering potted plants – the Peace Lily and the anthurium – on either side. "There, that looks good!" he said aloud. He placed the other luxuriantly leafed potted plants in corners that needed brightening up. Then he placed the tea chest in the little alcove in the passageway between the drawing room and the bedrooms. He found two wooden boards in the garage – left over from his renovation of the floor – and placed them across the top of the chest. After a few moments of consideration, he packed some books between two bookends and placed them on the boards. Then he looked around for a few small knick-knacks that would make the top of the old box look attractive. He wondered what it was about the rather battered old tea chest which drew him so. He read the stenciled writing again, then walked into his bedroom to fetch his laptop.

Sitting cross-legged on the floor beside the tea chest, he opened his laptop and typed in DOBBURI T.E. in the search bar. Immediately, options popped up, and he saw that the first one was the name of a company. Clicking that, he was led to the company's website and saw that it was a tea company. Dobburi was the name of one of the company's tea estates in Assam, a state in north-east India, according to the website. "So, T.E. must stand for tea estate," he thought.

Except for some statistics about location, size and yield, there wasn't much else about Dobburi Tea Estate on the website.

There was an email address given for the company's Head Office in Kolkata, India, so he made a note of it.

The next few days were busy ones at the University for Michael, as it was the middle of Term 1 of the first semester. When he was home, though, his eyes would go to the name stenciled in bold letters on the tea chest every time he passed it. He found himself giving the box an affectionate pat now and again. He sometimes found himself speaking to Lord Ganesh, as he now addressed the statue, after having read about him on the internet.

"Honestly, what's come over me?" he thought, shaking his head. "Living alone, with no one to talk to, I suppose."

His wife, Anthea, had died of cancer three years ago, and they had no children. Thinking of Anthea still created a tightness in his chest.

On Sunday, he got a call from Paul.

"Hey Michael," he said. "Dad says he knows someone at the London office of the tea company that the estate belongs to. Where your tea chest came from. His name's Gareth Twist. If you like, Dad can give Mr. Twist a call, and ask if you can get in touch with him. I'm sure he'll be able to tell you something about the estate and the tea chest."

For some reason, Michael felt a fluttering in his stomach. "That would be great, Paul," he said. "It's very kind of your dad to take the trouble."

The next evening, Michael received a message from Paul with Gareth Twist's phone number and email address. He thanked Paul and stared at the contact details contemplating whether he should email Mr. Twist right away or wait a few days.

"What are you waiting for, Michael?" he asked himself at last, and opening his laptop, started writing the email.

Michael rode into the premises of the University of Canterbury, just a fifteen-minute motorbike ride from his house in Burnside. He parked his Royal Enfield "Interceptor" and walked to the Karl Popper building, which housed the Social Sciences department. He took the lift to Level 6, where most of the faculty attached to the English Department had rooms. As he entered his room, he heard his mobile "ping." Dropping his jacket and helmet on a chair, he checked his phone and saw that he had a new email. It was from Mr. Twist.

It was polite but short, referring him to Mr. Surajit Guha, the General Manager at Dobburi Tea Estate, whose email address was given. "I know Surajit very well, and have told him to expect to hear from you. He can answer any questions you have about the estate. Regarding the tea chest you mention, 1991 was the last year that tea was packed in tea chests for export. Yours is therefore one of the last tea chests made," wrote Mr. Twist. He then ended the email sending his best regards.

Michael was pleasantly surprised by the promptness and helpfulness of Mr. Twist. He decided to make a list of his queries regarding his tea chest and Dobburi Tea Estate after returning home. Looking at his watch, he realized it was time for his first lecture of the day.

Getting back home that evening, Michael walked into his little foyer and dumped his bag, helmet, and jacket. He waved at Lord Ganesh and patted the tea chest on his way to his bedroom and bathroom. After washing up, he made himself a cup of tea, then sat with his laptop, thinking about the questions he wanted to ask Mr. Guha about Dobburi T.E.

***

Surajit read the email from Michael Fletcher. Gareth Twist had told him that a Dr Fletcher from Christchurch, New Zealand, would be getting in touch with him. Dr Fletcher wrote that he had got hold of an old tea chest which was originally packed with tea from Dobburi Tea Estate, and would like to know something about the estate. He was a diehard tea drinker but knew nothing about where the tea actually came from, how it was grown, and the process that changed the raw leaves into the product that was available in the market.

Tea planters are used to communicating with total strangers and even entertaining them as guests in their homes, so Surajit had no problem sending Dr Fletcher the information he had requested, but he was up to his neck in work as it was the beginning of the manufacturing season, and he was under tremendous pressure to produce best quality first flush teas. After thinking for a while, he forwarded the email to his wife, Indira. She was a writer, and her father had been General Manager of Dobburi for several years, so she had spent most of her teenage years there. Yes, she would be the best person to correspond with Dr Fletcher and tell him all about Dobburi Tea Estate, as she had actually spent more years on the estate than he, Surajit, had.

When he went home that evening, he asked Indira if she had read the email he had forwarded her. "Yes, I have," she replied, "But who's this Dr Fletcher, and why should I read his email?"

Surajit said, "He's a professor of English at Canterbury University in Christchurch, New Zealand, as he mentions in his email. He's got a tea chest which originally carried tea from here to England. He's intrigued and wants to know about the estate. Gareth referred him to me, but I don't have the time to gather all the information he wants and reply to his email. I'm responding to some fifty emails a day anyway – all work-related! On top of that, it's manufacturing season…"

"So, you want **me** to write to him, huh?" asked Indira.

"Darling, it would really help if you did. You've spent more years here than I have, anyway." He looked at her quizzically, and Indira burst out laughing.

She said, "If you could only see your expression! Such pleading puppy dog eyes! How could I resist?"

Surajit grinned and hugged her tight. "Have I told you today how much I love and appreciate you?" he asked.

"Emotional blackmail will get you everywhere, and you know it!" she replied, hugging him back and kissing the cleft on his chin.

Surajit sent Dr Fletcher a polite email saying that his wife, Indira, would be getting in touch with him and giving him all the information he wanted.

"She spent quite a few years on this estate earlier, as a teenager, when her father was the General Manager here," he wrote. "So, she knows a great deal about it. She is a writer, and will probably explain things much better than I could! She's also very interested in stories related to the tea estates."

***

Michael read the email from Surajit Guha, and replied saying it was indeed kind of Mrs. Guha to take the trouble and he was very grateful. He looked forward to hearing from her.

When he did receive the email from Indira Guha, he was pleasantly surprised by the detail she had gone into. She even sent him photographs of the estate, factory (but not inside, as that wasn't allowed, she explained), and the workers who had packed and sealed the tea chest!

"She must be a really good writer if she can make the description of a tea estate sound so interesting," he thought.

He wrote back, thanking her and asking if Dobburi tea was available in the market, but she replied saying that it was sold in bulk from the estate, and probably went into many brands.

"Do you know if it goes into Yorkshire Tea?" he asked, as that was his favorite brand.

"Yes, probably," replied Indira. Then she asked for his postal address, saying, "Surajit wants to send you a packet of Dobburi tea."

Michael was touched, and wrote, "That is so kind of Surajit. I really appreciate it."

When the packet of tea arrived, he placed the first spoonful into the tea chest, saying, "There you are!" He knew he was being sentimental but consoled himself thinking, "Well, no one's looking!" He found himself mentioning this little gesture to Indira, though, and asked, "Do you think it was a goofy thing to do?"

To which she replied, "Not at all! It was so appropriate! Just the right thing to do! Surajit thinks so too. He hopes you like the tea. First flush teas are coveted by connoisseurs of tea the world over." He replied saying it was the freshest and most aromatic tea he had ever tasted.

Over the next few months, he corresponded regularly with Indira and Surajit, finding he could write to them about every aspect of his life. Although it was Indira who wrote back, he knew that

Surajit read his emails too, because there was often a note from him at the end. When he mentioned that he had always wanted to visit India, they immediately invited him to visit Dobburi and stay with them for a few days. Indira even offered to make an itinerary for him if he sent her a list of the other places he wanted to visit in India.

Michael was overwhelmed by this generous offer. He couldn't believe that a few months ago, he hadn't even heard of Dobburi or the Guhas, and here they were, offering to host him! He felt that fluttering in his stomach again. "Why not?" he thought. He looked at Lord Ganesh's statue and asked, "What do you think? Should I accept their kind invitation?" The eyes seemed to twinkle at him. "I'm really getting fanciful!" he thought, grinning.

After he accepted their invitation and a few more emails were exchanged, Michael felt it was time to actually speak to Surajit and Indira over the phone. He asked if that was all right, and promptly got an email with both their phone numbers.

***

On a Sunday in December, Surajit stood outside the Arrivals gate of the airport, waiting for Michael. After a few minutes, the tall, lean, craggily handsome man he recognized from the video calls came striding out. When he saw Surajit, he broke into a huge grin, and came over to him, arm outstretched. They shook hands, exchanging pleasantries while the driver put Michael's luggage into the trunk of the car.

They spent the hour's drive chatting, and Surajit told Michael what he and Indira had planned for him during his stay. "Sounds great!" said Michael. "I can't thank you both enough."

Surajit waved away his thanks, saying, "Not at all. It's your first trip to India, and to the home of your tea chest, so we want it to be memorable."

As they entered the estate, Michael saw the signboard saying "Dobburi Tea Estate" and felt the fluttering again in his stomach. Driving through the gates of the bungalow, he stared admiringly at the gracious two-storied structure set to one side of a large green lawn bordered with flower beds filled with a variety and profusion of flowers.

Indira was waiting in the verandah, and greeted him with a warm handshake.

"How was your flight? Are you jetlagged?" she asked while he drank the glass of water offered him by a man in white uniform.

"It was fine, but yes, I am a little jetlagged, though very excited to be here," he replied.

Surajit excused himself, saying he'd see Michael in about fifteen minutes, and Indira led the way to the guestroom. She stopped at the door and said, "This is your room. Your luggage is in the dressing room attached, and the bathroom is just off the dressing room. Once you've freshened up, will you come to the verandah? Lunch will be served in another fifteen minutes. Is that all right?"

Michael thanked her, saying that would be fine, and entered the beautifully laid out room. He suddenly felt a bit dizzy and blamed it on jetlag.

"I should rest a bit after lunch," he thought. Surajit and Indira gave him the same advice.

When Michael came out to the verandah after his nap, he found Indira and Surajit sitting there. Surajit smiled and asked, "Did you sleep? Are you feeling rested?"

Michael sat on one of the chairs and said, "Yes, thank you." Indira asked if he'd like a cup of tea, to which he replied, "Yes, please! I'd love a cup of Dobburi tea!"

Then he handed them the gifts he'd brought for them – a scarf, paua shell earrings and a diary for Indira, a cap, a desk calendar and a diary for Surajit, a set of coasters with paua shell inlays, different kinds of cheese and Tim Tams.

"Oh, my goodness! That's a lot of goodies! And my favorite Tim Tams!" exclaimed Indira. "How kind of you, Michael, thank you so much!"

Surajit thanked him warmly too. He tried on the black cap with the New Zealand fern embroidered on it in white.

"Very smart," said Indira. "I've got the ferns on my scarf too!"

Surajit said, "We thought you could rest this evening. We've organized a bit of entertainment for you, though." The entertainment turned out to be a folk song and dance performance by a group of workers. Michael found the song, the drumbeat and the footwork of the dancers mesmerizing.

The next morning, after breakfast, Surajit took Michael for a drive around the estate in his Gypsy – a sturdy, four-wheel drive vehicle used by most Managers of tea estates. He showed Michael the bushes of different ages, explaining that old, unproductive tea bushes were uprooted and replanted with healthy new saplings.

"After rehabilitating the soil, of course. We use Guatemala grass for that." He showed Michael some sections of the estate planted with the grass, and explained the whole process of preparing the soil for the new saplings.

Then they went to the factory, where Surajit showed him the machinery and explained the whole process of tea manufacture. Michael found all of it fascinating, though, being winter, there was no actual manufacturing going on.

He was introduced to the two workers who had packed his box with tea and sealed it. Surajit explained that sealing a tea chest was a specialist task, as the nails had to go in very precisely at regular intervals. Michael shook their hands, very pleased to meet the two men directly connected with his tea chest. Surajit took a photograph of him standing with them.

"We don't use tea chests anymore, though, as you know," said Surajit, "So they both have other jobs now."

When they went home for lunch, Indira told them that she had located the oldest retired worker on the estate, an 85-year-old man called Birbal Bhumij. She asked Surajit if their driver could pick Birbal up from his home and bring him to the bungalow in the Gypsy at 3.30pm. "I'm sure he'll have some stories and anecdotes about the estate's past, which might interest Michael," she said.

Surajit agreed, and called the driver to give him the "kamjari," which Michael now knew translated to "task."

Michael rested after lunch again, then went out to the verandah and had a cup of tea with Indira, who told him that Surajit had gone back to work. When they heard the Gypsy entering the bungalow a few minutes later, Indira said, "Let's go downstairs. There's a small sitting room there."

Indira greeted Birbal respectfully in the local patois (as she explained to Michael). "He is most comfortable speaking in the language of the tea estate workers. It's a kind of pidgin – a mix of a few languages from different parts of India. Having grown up in the tea estates, I speak it fluently, so I'll translate."

Michael thanked her and greeted the old man with folded hands, saying "Namaste!" He was a little disconcerted to find the old man staring at him fixedly.

Then Birbal addressed him directly, saying a word that sounded like "I-gully." Nonplussed, Michael looked enquiringly at Indira.

"He said 'you've come,' like he was expecting you. He also addressed you as someone familiar," she explained, a little startled herself. "Perhaps he's mistaken you for someone else."

She asked the old man gently, "Do you know him? Were you expecting him?"

Birbal nodded and said, "I knew he would come one day. That's why I couldn't die. I had to wait for him."

As Indira translated this for Michael, Birbal looked at Michael and smiled fondly. Taken aback, Michael looked helplessly at Indira.

Birbal said, "His father, Willis Sahab, was my Sahab. I was his personal servant and looked after him from the day he joined this estate. But, sadly, three years later, after coming back from leave from his own country, he fell ill and died. I was so sad. It was as if I had lost my brother. Before dying, he told me, 'Birbal, I am engaged to a lovely girl, Anna. Something happened between us which shouldn't have. Not before marriage, that is, but now I'm glad it did. At least I know what it is to love and be loved by a woman. She and her mother were supposed to come here this winter, and we were going to be married here. But now, I'll never see Anna again." He started weeping as if his heart were breaking. My own heart was breaking for my Sahab, and I knew he wouldn't survive, but I still tried to console him and lift up his spirits."

The old man wiped his eyes with his scarf. Michael had been listening uncomprehendingly, but when he heard the name "Anna," he was startled. That had been his mother's name! He looked at Indira enquiringly, and she explained what Birbal had said.

Michael said, "I don't know anyone called Willis, but my mother's name was Anna."

Hearing the name, Birbal repeated, "Anna, Anna! Tor Ma?"

Michael understood the word "Ma." He nodded.

Birbal turned to Indira and explained, "After my Sahab died, I tried to give his box of letters and photographs to the Burra Sahab, asking if he would send it to his family, but the Burra Sahab said that Willis Sahab's family had said they didn't want anything of his to be sent home. I think they were afraid his things would carry the disease to them or something! His clothes were divided among all his servants, but the Burra Sahab gave me my Sahab's watch. He told me to burn the letters and photographs, but I couldn't do it. My heart told me that one day, someone would come to claim that box and its contents. And see, today, my Sahab's son has come."

When Indira translated, Michael was bemused. "My father's name was Ted Fletcher. He never set foot in India. He and my mother left England for New Zealand when I was just about a year old. We lived there ever since. My parents have both passed on now. My mother's name was Anna, but I've never heard the name Willis. Was it his first name or surname?" asked Michael.

Indira relayed the question to Birbal, but the old man just shook his head. Then he asked if the driver could take him home to bring the box. Indira called the driver and told him to take the old man home, and then bring him back. She was intrigued by the story but didn't say anything to Michael, who was looking a bit thoughtful.

"I think I'll call my aunt, Belle. She's my mother's twin sister who lives in Sussex, England. Let's see if my mother knew anyone called Willis."

Indira nodded, and left the room to give him some privacy.

After around fifteen minutes, she heard Michael call her name. He sounded strange, so she hurried in. He was slumped in one of the armchairs, looking pale and shellshocked.

She walked to him quickly and asked, "Are you alright? You look kind of pale." She poured him a glass of water from the carafe on the table.

He gulped the water and said, "My aunt was absolutely stunned to know where I was! She didn't remember the name of this estate, but she certainly knew Steve Willis whom my mother was engaged to! It seems that my mother was pregnant by him when he returned to India and died. Desperate, she told Aunt Belle, who advised her to marry my father, I mean Ted Fletcher, who was a few years older than both of them, and also in love with my mother. My mother insisted on telling Ted the truth and he told her he would marry her on the condition that I never be told who my real father was. It hardly mattered, as my real father was dead. No one else but the three of them knew the truth. Of course, there was some talk as I was born prematurely. To get away from the speculation and gossip, my parents decided to migrate to New Zealand. They might have been afraid I would start to look like Steve. He had lived in the same neighborhood, so most of the people had known him."

Indira sat on the armchair next to Michael's and looked at him with sympathy. Imagine coming on holiday to another country and finding out by chance that your biological father was someone else!

"I'm so sorry. I precipitated all this by calling Birbal over," she said apologetically.

"No, no!" exclaimed Michael. "Yes, it's a shock, but at least I know the truth about my parentage. How fortunate that you thought of bringing old Birbal to meet me! If you hadn't, I wouldn't have known any of this."

She asked him gently, "But do you feel you might've been better off not knowing?"

Michael said thoughtfully, "Honestly, I feel the opposite. I was probably meant to know. That's why I found the tea chest. I saw the name of this estate, and wanted to know more about it. I got in touch with Mr. Twist, who put me in touch with Surajit and you, and that eventually brought me here. Perhaps the time was right, so it all fell into place." He sank into thought again.

"If you don't mind my asking, was Ted a good father?" asked Indira hesitantly.

"Yes, he was," replied Michael. "I was closer to him than I was to my mother. She always seemed to be holding back. She had this habit of looking at me searchingly when she thought no one was looking. It used to puzzle me, but now I know why." They sat in silence again, but after a while Michael apologized saying, "I'm sorry. It's just a lot to take in."

Indira said gently, "There's no need to apologize, Michael. I understand what a shock it is to you. It must be so surreal to know that you aren't who you thought you were all these years." Michael nodded, grateful for her understanding.

After a while, they heard the sound of the vehicle returning, so Indira stepped out to escort Birbal back in. The old man was holding an old cigar box as if it were made of gold. He held it out to Michael who took it slowly.

"How are you so sure that Michael is Willis Sahab's son?" asked Indira curiously.

Birbal indicated the box, which Michael was opening hesitantly. He saw letters addressed to Steve Willis in his mother's handwriting from her younger days. Under those, there were some old black and white photographs. When he looked at the face in one of them, he saw the resemblance to himself when he was in his twenties. He knew he was looking at his father. He passed it to Indira. Then he looked at a photograph of his father with, presumably, his parents. The older man, his grandfather, looked much as Michael did now. No wonder Birbal had recognized him as Steve Willis' son!

He looked at Birbal, who was smiling at him with tears in his eyes. This old man, a stranger halfway across the world, had kept his father's precious possessions in safe custody, waiting for the day someone would claim them. Such simple faith! He went up to Birbal and gently held the old man's hands in both of his.

Indira suddenly exclaimed, "Michael, your father must be buried somewhere here!"

She asked Birbal. The old man nodded. He said Steve Willis was buried by the riverside just below the football field. The Manager at that time, had arranged for a headstone but that had broken during an earthquake, and slowly disintegrated over the years.

"I used to keep the area around the grave clean but now it must be overgrown because I can't go there anymore. It's too long a walk for me."

Indira translated and said, "I know the place. As a teenager, I used to wonder whose grave it was!"

Michael was almost too overcome to speak. What a faithful friend the old man had been even after Steve's death! He swallowed hard and managed to ask Indira, "Could we go and see the grave now?"

Indira hesitated, then said gently, "It's already dark, Michael, and there won't be lights there. I know you want to go now, but I think it would be better to go tomorrow morning. You'll be able to see better."

Michael knew what she said made sense, so he nodded. Indira asked Birbal which bungalow Steve Willis had occupied.

"I'm sure you'd like to see where your father lived too," she said to Michael, who nodded again.

She asked Birbal whether Steve Willis had died in his bungalow or in the hospital. To her surprise, he replied that Steve had died in this bungalow!

"When it became clear that he wouldn't live much longer, the Burra Sahab brought him here, and put him up in the guest room, where I looked after him. The Memsahab was very kind. She made sure he had chicken soup, milk, and other nutritious drinks. He couldn't eat solid food towards the end."

When Indira translated this for Michael, saying that his father had spent the last few days of his life in the room he was presently occupying, he remembered the slight dizziness he had felt on entering the room for the first time. He felt goose bumps now.

Indira offered Birbal tea and snacks, then asked the driver to drop him home. Michael asked Indira to take a photograph of him with Birbal. Then he asked her to convey his heartfelt thanks to the old man. "Both for taking care of my father so faithfully when he was alive, and for introducing me to him."

Birbal caressed his arm lovingly before leaving. "Baba," he said. Michael felt the tears surge in his eyes.

"Baba is what we call our father, but it's also an endearment we use for our sons," explained Indira. "It's what all the household staff call the son of the house too." Michael was too choked to reply.

After Birbal left, Michael excused himself and went up to his room. He sat in an armchair and stared at the cigar box in his hands. He opened it slowly and took out the photographs, studying them properly. Apart from the one of Steve alone, and the one of Steve with his parents, there was a small one of Michael's mother smiling shyly. She had signed it 'With all my love, Anna." The last one was of a group of young people at a party, He recognized Steve, his mother, Aunt Belle and the man he had known as his father – Ted Fletcher. How young they looked! Steve and his mother were smiling at each other, while Ted looked on with a small frown. Belle was talking to another young man. Looking closer, he recognized her husband, his Uncle Ben. He stared at the photograph for a long time. A moment frozen in time. Little did his parents or Ted know then what life had in store for them. He was overcome with sorrow for Steve, dying so young, for Anna, pregnant and losing her fiancé, and for Ted who may have felt he came second to a dead man in his wife's affections.

He thought back to his parents' marriage. He didn't remember them quarrelling, although they did have arguments. They had similar tastes and got along well. He came to the conclusion that Anna may have married Ted out of compulsion, but she had grown to love him. He wondered why they hadn't had any children, though. Now that he knew the truth of his parentage, he was overcome with love and respect for Ted.

"He will always remain my father. He was the one who loved me and brought me up. Gave me the best of everything," he thought, with gratitude. He remembered his father's pride when he had got his doctorate.

"Perhaps Steve would have been a good father too, if he'd had the chance, but I'll never know. What I do know is that Ted was a wonderful father. He made life interesting and fun," he thought.

He looked at the bundle of letters from his mother to Steve. There were around a dozen of them.

"I suppose letters took months to reach India from England those days, and the same time from India to England. So, a dozen would be around three years' worth of letters," he thought.

He noticed that one of the envelopes was still sealed. It must have arrived after Steve's death, and Birbal must have kept it in the box with the rest of the letters. He was tempted to tear open the envelope and read the last letter, guessing his mother may have told Steve about her pregnancy. But he couldn't do it.

There was a small object wrapped in gauze in one corner of the box. He unwrapped it carefully and found he was holding an idol of Ganesh carved in black stone! Michael stared at the figurine for the longest time, staggered by the coincidence.

"What other things did we have in common, Father?" he asked silently.

The last object in the box was a fountain pen. Michael wondered if that had been a gift from his mother. He put everything back in the box and laid it on the table by his side. Then he sat lost in thought.

When Surajit came home from work he asked Indira, "So, did the old man have any good stories to tell?"

Indira took a deep breath and said, "An extraordinary one, actually!"

Surajit was stunned when he heard the story. Then he quickly made a phone call to his Senior Assistant Manager, Ajai Singh, telling him about Steve Willis' grave, and where it was located. "There may be a lot of overgrown grass and plants, and remnants of an old headstone. Just have it cleaned up early tomorrow morning. Ask the carpenter to make a nice wooden cross with RIP carved on it, and place it at one end. My guest will be visiting it after breakfast tomorrow to pay his respects. Make sure it's all done by then, please. Oh, and Ajai, please tell Vivek I'll be taking my guest to see his bungalow sometime tomorrow. I'll fix the time later. Thanks." As he disconnected, he could almost feel the static vibrating with the questions Ajai was too polite to ask.

Michael roused himself and went to join Surajit and Indira in the drawing room. He smiled wryly at Surajit and said, "You must have heard."

"Yes," replied Surajit. "I'm blown away! Just imagine! You found an old tea chest lying in someone's garden shed in New Zealand, and it led you to your biological father here, in India!" He shook his head in amazement.

Michael said, "From the very beginning, I was drawn to the tea chest. You won't believe this, but I pat it every time I pass by it! When I got in touch with Mr. Twist, I felt a fluttering in my stomach. You know, like when you're nervous. I didn't understand why. I got the same feeling when I came here. I am not extra sensitive or anything like that, but this affinity with the tea chest – actually with the name, Dobburi – was something I've never experienced before. I was compelled by some force outside myself to find out as much as I could about it."

Indira quoted Hamlet, saying, "There are more things in heaven and earth, Horatio, than are dreamt of in your philosophy."

Michael smiled absently, saying, "Yes, Shakespeare can be so relevant, even after centuries!"

Later that night, as he lay in bed, Michael remembered the saying, "Truth is stranger than fiction." He had never given it much thought but now he realized how true it was. He was sleeping in the same room, and perhaps on the same bed, that his father had occupied and died in. What were the chances of such a thing happening? He thought of Surajit's comment about an old tea chest in New Zealand leading him to his father in faraway India. No matter how pragmatic a person might be, he had to wonder at such coincidences.

He wondered if he should feel some resentment towards Ted for keeping his paternity a secret. Perhaps he would have, had he been younger. But he understood Ted's motive and knew he had thought it would be in Michael's best interests to believe Ted was his father. It had certainly made Michael's life simple and contented.

He sat up and reached out for the cigar box which he'd placed on the bedside table. Opening it, he took out the photographs and looked at each one of them again. Then he put them away and took out his mother's last letter. He passed his fingers over the flap of the envelope again and again, but finally put that away too. He switched off the bedside lamp and lay down. Although his head was still buzzing with thoughts, he was emotionally exhausted and soon fell asleep.

After breakfast the next morning, Surajit took him to see his father's grave. Indira hesitated, not wanting to intrude, but Michael insisted she accompany them too. She had plucked some flowers from the garden and made a beautiful bouquet. She also carried a scented candle and a box of matches with her. Michael was touched by her thoughtfulness.

He had expected to see an untidy tangle of weeds and overgrown vegetation around his father's grave, but was stunned to see a beautifully clean grave with an edging of whitewashed boulders and a brand new wooden cross at one end. He looked at Surajit with gratitude. Indira handed him the bouquet, which he placed on the grave. Then he lit the candle and placed it beneath the cross. At Michael's request, Surajit took a few pictures, then walked away with Indira, leaving him alone.

Michael stood at his father's grave, his mind a blank. Then, from somewhere, the words of a prayer came to him. He said them silently. Then, after one last look, he turned away and walked back to the vehicle, joining Surajit and Indira who were waiting for him. He looked at them both, his heart full of gratitude towards this warm and wonderful couple who had probably done more for him in the last few months and especially in these last three days than anyone else had done in his fifty-three years. For a professor of English and Creative Writing, he was strangely bereft of words. All he could say was, simply, "Thank you." Surajit patted his arm and Indira smiled at him warmly.

Back at the bungalow, Michael asked Surajit if he could pay for a headstone to be placed at his father's grave.

"Of course!" replied Surajit. "In fact, I was already planning to get one made, and ask you what you'd like inscribed on it."

Michael was touched by Surajit's thoughtfulness. "I'll think about the inscription and let you know," he replied. He also told Surajit that he would like to look after Birbal for as long as he was alive. "May I send you a certain sum every month to give him?" he asked.

Surajit said, "Of course. I'll make sure he gets it. Mind you, I can do that for as long as I'm here. But when I get transferred, I'll have to make other arrangements. Anyway, I should be here for another three years, hopefully. After that, we'll see."

Michael said, "I am so glad I took up your offer and came here now, while Birbal is still alive. If I had waited a year or two, who knows if he'd still have been alive. I might never have known about my biological father. And I'm eternally grateful to Indira for calling Birbal to the bungalow." Then he added, "Would it be possible for me to meet him again? I'd like to know more about my father."

Surajit said, "Of course! I'll have it arranged."

Michael thanked him and the two men sat in easy silence, both lost in thought, till Indira entered and announced that lunch was served. "Another sumptuous feast!" exclaimed Michael, following Indira to the dining room, with Surajit close behind.

The next few days were filled with new experiences for Michael. Surajit and Indira took him to the club. Although he hadn't played tennis in years, he managed to put up a creditable performance as Surajit's doubles partner. The other tea planters and their wives were warm and friendly. There were many invitations to lunch, tea and dinner.

Before leaving for Mumbai at the end of an eventful ten days, Michael repeated his invitation to Surajit and Indira, to visit him in Christchurch. "Promise me you'll come soon." They assured him they would.

"Anyway, we'll be in touch," said Surajit. "Let us know when you've reached home safely."

Michael said, "Of course!" He hugged them both warmly, thanking them again for everything, especially for the two packets of Dobburi tea.

***

Michael paid off the taxi and pulled his suitcase to his front door. Unlocking it, he entered the foyer, dumping his suitcase there. Then he drew back the curtains and opened the windows in all the rooms.

"From winter to summer in a matter of hours!" thought Michael. A lovely, warm breeze blew in, freshening the air inside the house.

He looked at Lord Ganesh fondly and said, "Well, I've just returned from your beautiful country. But then you'd know that, wouldn't you?"

Then he stood in front of the tea chest, lightly running his fingers across the letters spelling out "Dobburi Tea Estate."

"And you… you took me on a journey of discovery, didn't you?"

He walked into his bedroom, looked at Anthea's photograph and said, "I'm home."

He unlocked his suitcase and took out his father's cigar box, placing it on the wooden board on top of the tea chest. He took out the stone idol of Ganesh and kept it in front of the books. He'd leave the pen and letters in the box, but frame the photographs. He wondered if he could ever bring himself to read the letters. Perhaps not all, but he might eventually read the last one, in which his mother had probably informed Steve of Michael's conception.

The next day, he drove to the garden center to collect his plants which Paul had been looking after in his absence. As he alighted from his truck, Paul hailed him. "Hi Michael!" he called. "So, how was your trip to India? Find anything interesting in that tea estate your old tea chest came from?"

Michael thought of Surajit and Indira, of loyal Birbal, of his young father dying in a distant land, his young mother pregnant and scared, and of the man who had, to all intents and purposes, been his father. Michael wondered what Paul's reaction would be if he said, "Yes. I found two good friends; a loyal old man; my biological father and my real identity; deeper love, respect and admiration for the man I knew as my father; and compassion and understanding for my mother. And my life has been enriched by it all."

He smiled and said mildly, "Yes, it was interesting," and left it at that, because some things are best left unsaid and some secrets are best kept forever.

The Great Revenge

Sometimes, compassion may be the greatest revenge!

Anne leaned closer to her mother who was struggling to tell her something. "Mum," she said gently to the wasted woman lying on the hospital bed. "What is it? Can't you tell me when you're feeling better?"

"No!" said the older woman as strongly as she could. "I've got to tell you now, while I can. Perhaps I should have told you this earlier. Or perhaps I shouldn't tell you at all, but I can't keep this secret any longer. I can't take it to my grave."

Although Anne knew her mother was dying, she automatically said, "You are not going to your grave just yet, Mum. You'll get better and come home."

Her mother looked at her with infinite sorrow and compassion and gave her a ghost of her lovely smile.

"All right, Mum. What is this great secret that you've been keeping from me?" Anne asked indulgently. She couldn't imagine her gentle mother having some ominous secret. But suddenly her mother seemed tongue-tied. "What is it, Mum?" Anne asked again.

Cathy gathered all her pitiful strength and said, "It's about your father."

***

In the late 1950s, Oliver Munroe had been a sailor on a ship, but had left the ship in Calcutta, India, when one of the passengers had offered him a well-paid job in a tea estate in Assam. He had taken up the job and loved it from the start. He had also loved all the sports that tea planters played – polo, tennis, cricket and golf – but shooting turned out to be his forte. He was such a good shot that he was granted a license by the authorities to shoot rogue elephants and man-eating tigers that attacked the tea estates and villages which adjoined forests.

Anne didn't remember her father but had heard stories about him from her mother. Her father had died, ironically enough, in a freak shooting accident when she was only four years old. Cathy had brought Anne back to England, where they had made their home with Cathy's parents in West Sussex. Cathy, who had been a teacher before marrying Oliver and going to India, soon found a teaching job in the local school. Anne studied at the same school, and they stayed with her grandparents until Cathy married a colleague, Peter Woods.

Peter was a talented pianist and composer, and a wonderful teacher. Anne was one of her step-father's students, and appreciated his immense patience. He was the only father she had known and she loved him whole-heartedly. Though not an overly demonstrative man, she knew he loved her too. His whole face lit up the first time she called him "Dad."

Anne studied Library Science and got a job as Librarian in the town library. She met a visiting professor from Stanford called Adam Sheldon, fell in love, married him, and moved to USA, but divorced him amicably after five years and returned to England with her three-year-old daughter, Sarah. Although Adam kept in touch in the beginning, father and daughter had grown somewhat distant over the years, especially when he remarried and had another family. Sarah hardly went to visit him but they did speak over the phone once a month.

When Sarah was six, Anne married her old classmate, Mark Ainsley, and they moved to Wimbledon, London, where Mark was an official at the All England Lawn Tennis and Croquet Club – or just "Wimbledon" as it was known.

Mark was a great step-father, and always claimed with a wink and his infectious grin that he'd married Anne just to get Sarah as a daughter. Ben had been born after a couple of years.

Mark treated Sarah and Ben with the same love and affection, and was equally strict with both when they were children and teenagers. Not that they needed to be disciplined very often, as Sarah was a quiet girl, spending most of her time in the library where her mother worked, and Ben was on the tennis courts at Wimbledon every day after school. So, they were usually under the eye of one of their parents when they weren't in school. The odd transgression of coming home late or slightly tipsy as a teenager was dealt with very sensibly and without undue drama. Sarah knew she and Ben were fortunate to have exceptional parents. The very apparent love between Anne and Mark made their home a happy one.

The eight-year gap between Sarah and Ben meant that, once she was old enough, Ben was left in Sarah's care whenever their parents went out, unless she had plans of her own. The siblings ended up spending a great deal of time together. Over the years, the age gap ceased to matter, and they grew closer.

Ben was now a professional tennis player and the newest hope for England. He had quite a fan following, especially among young girls, but behind that handsome face and charming manner, he was a practical, grounded, and determined young man.

***

Now Anne asked her mother, "What did you want to tell me about Dad, Mum?"

Peter had died of a heart attack five years ago, and she still missed him very much.

Cathy hesitated again, then said hoarsely, "He was murdered." She closed her eyes as if physically and emotionally exhausted.

Anne thought she couldn't have heard right. Peter, murdered? Her mother's mind must be wandering because of the heavy medication. "What did you say, Mum?" she asked.

Cathy opened her eyes and whispered, "Your father, Oliver, was murdered."

Not Peter. Oliver. Anne was stunned. After a few minutes, she managed to ask, "Why? By whom?"

***

Anne unlocked the front door of her house and walked in as if in a dream. She plonked down on the sofa and leaned back. She played her mother's words back in her head like a record, but her main thought was, "He was killed for nothing! Nothing!" It was like a refrain popping up in the midst of other thoughts.

***

The Manager of the estate where Oliver was posted was a tall, big redhead called Harris McIntosh. He had a booming voice and a loud laugh. He was a kind man and good at his job, but not overly bright or charming. He was also short-tempered, though his anger faded as quickly as it flashed.

"It's the red hair," he explained to Oliver ruefully.

Oliver was fond of him, as was Cathy. When Harris was in his forties, he went to England on leave, married a lovely girl in her late twenties called Barbara, and brought her back to Assam. The bride was welcomed by everyone, and she and Cathy soon became friends. Harris asked Cathy to show Barbara "the ropes," which Cathy did tactfully.

A couple of years later, Victor Preston arrived in the district. He was posted as Manager of the estate neighboring Mihirjan, where Harris and Oliver worked. Victor was handsome, charming and a bachelor at fifty.

"Never met the right woman!" he said when people asked him why he wasn't married. "Until now," he could have added.

When he met Barbara for the very first time at the local club, he fell deeply in love with her, and she with him. It was something they didn't need to express in words. They looked at each other and just knew. It was like recognizing the other half of yourself that you didn't know was missing.

It wasn't easy to have a secret affair in the tea estates, where there were eyes everywhere, but they managed to send notes to each other through his trusted manservant and her personal maid, and met in a remote corner of Mihirjan that shared a common boundary with Victor's estate. She would cycle there while he drove in his Jeep. They were always wary of being seen by an estate worker passing by, so all they could do was hold hands and talk, and exchange the occasional kiss.

"We have to think of a way to be together without hurting or humiliating Harris too badly," said Victor. "You know how people gossip." Barbara was silent, thinking of Harris' temper. "I'll look for a job in another company, preferably one which has estates in Dooars or the Barak valley, where Harris' company doesn't have estates," continued Victor. "When I leave, you can go back to England and divorce Harris. I'll come to England on my next annual leave and we'll get married. Does that sound like a plan?"

Barbara nodded and leaned her head on his shoulder. "People will still gossip about us. Tea is a small community," she said softly.

"It'll be a nine days' wonder, Darling. Something or someone else will come along, giving the gossips new grist for their mill. We'll soon become a staid old couple," he said bracingly.

At social events, Victor was strictly circumspect with Barbara, treating her with the same charming respect as the other ladies. But Harris started suspecting that something was going on between Barbara and another man, because try as she would, she couldn't help being a little distant with him. When she shrank away from his touch, he was sure. He didn't suspect Victor, who was older than him and therefore, he felt, too old for Barbara. He wondered who it could be, watching her with the younger men at the club and at parties.

Finally deciding to take the bull by the horns, Harris confronted Barbara, demanding that she tell him who she was having an affair with. She realized it would be fruitless to deny it, but fearing his temper, and trying to shield Victor from it, she blurted out Oliver's name. She immediately regretted it, knowing it had been a blunder, because Harris would storm off and confront him. Of course, Oliver would deny it, but what would he think of her? But Harris was uncharacteristically calm. He stared at her for a few seconds, then turned on his heel and left, leaving her gaping after him in dismay. What on earth had made her say Oliver's name? What a stupid thing to have done!

Biting her lip, she thought she had to send Victor a message, asking him to come over that evening, so that they could talk to Harris together. She needed his support. She couldn't keep on living with Harris, especially now that he knew she was having an affair. That sounded so tawdry! Victor was the love of her life, and she was his. The irony was that they might never have met if she hadn't married Harris and come to Assam! Life could play such jokes on one sometimes.

That same afternoon, Harris received a message from the Manager of an estate adjoining the forest ten kilometers away, saying that a rogue elephant had killed a man in the neighboring village and had been seen making its way towards his estate. Harris was requested to send Oliver to hunt it down. Harris informed Oliver and offered to drive him there, so around 6 PM, they drove out together.

Only one man returned alive – Harris. Distraught and disheveled, he brought back Oliver's body, shot by his own gun. According to Harris, the rogue elephant had suddenly loomed in front of them in the mist, and Oliver had hurriedly pulled the trigger. Instead of hitting the elephant, the bullet had hit a tree, ricocheted and hit Oliver in the chest, killing him instantly.

No one had any reason to disbelieve Harris' story, so that was the official account given to the authorities and Oliver's death was ruled as "accidental."

A grieving Cathy did wonder vaguely why Barbara looked so pale and scared, but she soon left India with Anne, and that was the end of the chapter for her.

***

Two years ago, Cathy had received a letter forwarded to her by Harris' solicitors after his death, in which he had confessed to killing Oliver because Barbara had told him that she was having an affair with him. "I realized later that she had lied. It was Victor. He was waiting with her when I returned with Oliver's body. She left me and came back to England soon after the incident. Then she divorced me and married him. If only she had told me the truth! I was so fond of Oliver. After his death, and especially after I realized he had been innocent, I was never the same. I couldn't stay in Assam any longer. In fact, I left India and joined a tea company in Ceylon. I cannot find the words to apologize to you and Anne. I do not expect your forgiveness because I do not deserve it. I can't even blame Barbara. It was my decision to take a life. But it wasn't planned, believe me. It happened on the spur of the moment."

He went on to describe what had happened, and expressed his regrets over and over again.

Cathy was devastated. She had grieved for Oliver all those years ago, but now she grieved anew. To have been murdered, and that too, for no fault of his! Because of a woman's lie! She found that she could forgive Harris but not Barbara. If she had come face to face with her, she didn't know what she would have done! The woman had deprived Cathy of her husband and Anne of her father, for no reason at all. Cathy didn't know what to do. Should she tell Anne? After a great deal of consideration, Cathy had kept the knowledge to herself. Until now. Face to face with death herself, she knew Anne had to know the truth.

***

The funeral and wake were over. Sarah helped Mark and Ben clear the table and wash the dishes. Mark asked, "Are you sure you won't stay the night, Love? Your room is always kept ready for you, you know that, don't you?"

Sarah nodded and hugged him. How fortunate she was to have Mark as a step-father!

"Thanks Dad, but I have to go home. Early day tomorrow." Sarah was a geriatrician. She shared a practice with two other geriatric specialists, and visited a retirement home on a regular basis. "I have to go to Peace Haven tomorrow, which is a longish drive, then be back in time for my afternoon appointments."

She hugged her brother. "Bye, Brat," she said affectionately, tousling his hair. "All the best for your match on Saturday. I'll be there to cheer you on."

Ben thanked her and kissed her cheek affectionately. "Drive carefully," he said.

She walked to her parents' room and knocked gently on the door. "Come in," called Anne. Sarah walked to the bed and sat beside her mother, who was lying down.

"How are you feeling, Mum?" she asked gently. She touched Anne's cheek with a loving hand.

"Tired. I miss your Gran," sighed Anne.

"So do I," said Sarah, and clasping her mother's hand, kissed it.

Anne's eyes brimmed with tears. Then she said softly. "Darling, I have to show you something."

She slipped her hand under her pillow and handed Sarah the letter Harris had written to Cathy. "This must be kept between you and me. At least for now. I don't want to upset Mark and Ben, and distract Ben so close to the Championship."

Cathy had slipped into a coma the day after she had told Anne the truth, and died a week later. The letter was among Cathy's papers, so Anne took it and kept it with her. In it, Harris described how he had looked for any signs of remorse or embarrassment in Oliver's demeanor as they'd waited to sight the rogue elephant. Eventually, when he hadn't detected the slightest signs of either, Harris had become inflamed with rage at what he had thought of as Oliver's effrontery and lack of shame. His sense of betrayal was worsened by his liking and affection for Oliver. Overcome by outrage and fury, he had seized Oliver's gun from the ground and fired at him. He wrote that he could never forget the expression of shock and puzzlement on Oliver's face just before the bullet hit him and took his life.

Anne was not only grieving for Cathy, but also trying to process the new information about her father's death. Not an accident but murder!

Now, as Sarah read the letter, she was overcome with sadness and anger too, thinking, "So, Oliver was murdered, and for no reason! How could this Barbara woman be so wicked?"

She squeezed her mother's hand and looked at her with deep compassion. She imagined how she would feel if Mark, or

Adam, died, and she mourned him, only to come to know many years later that someone had murdered him for no reason.

"Would you like me to stay, Mum?" she asked.

Anne shook her head. "No, Darling. You go on home. I know you have an early start tomorrow. I'll be fine."

Sarah kissed her mother and said, "I'll call you. And I'm coming back next weekend. Then we'll talk." Anne nodded and kissed her back.

During the drive home, Sarah went over Harris' letter in her mind. Her heart was wrenched by the futility of her grandfather's death.

She hadn't said anything to Anne, but her mind was churning. Harris, her grandfather's murderer, was dead, but she had to find out where Barbara was. Victor would probably be dead by now. Anyway, she wasn't interested in him. In her eyes, Barbara was her grandfather's real killer. She had to find Barbara. She hoped the woman was still alive. Once she found her, she would confront her. See if she was remorseful. Then she would decide what to do next.

After getting home, she made herself a cup of tea. She knew her grandmother and mother weren't members of any tea planters' groups on social media, but her grandmother had friends who were. "That's where I'll start," she thought.

The next day, she called her grandmother's "tea" friends, Julia Smith and Mary Davies, and thanked them for their flowers and messages of condolence. Julia had gone to visit her daughter in France and Mary was at her grandson's wedding in Scotland. She chatted with each for a while, and casually asked about Barbara. She told them that Cathy had left a memento for Barbara, so she, Sarah, was trying to get in touch with her. They seemed surprised but were too polite to say so. Both promised to find out what they could.

The next two weeks flew by as Sarah had two emergencies at Peace Haven in addition to her regular workload. She managed to go to Wimbledon over the weekend but didn't get a chance to talk to her mother alone. On Saturday, they watched Ben play and win a match, and then celebrated over dinner. On Sunday, Mark's sister and family came over for lunch. By the time they left, it was time for Sarah to leave too.

Getting back home late that evening, she received a phone call from Julia Smith. "Sarah, darling," said Julia, sounding excited. "I've got some news!"

"What is it, Aunt Julia?" asked Sarah. (She had always addressed Julia and Mary as "Aunt" following the "tea" tradition taught to her by her grandmother).

"Barbara McIntosh… I mean… Preston, lives in Shillong, in India. Victor worked till he was in his mid-sixties, then retired and settled in Shillong. It's a lovely town up in the hills in the state of Meghalaya in eastern India. We used to all go there for short holidays, to get away from the heat of Assam. Until sometime in the early 1970s, if memory serves, Shillong was actually the capital of Assam."

"So, the Prestons live in this town, Shillong," reconfirmed Sarah.

"Victor died some years ago, so Barbara lives there alone now," replied Julia.

Sarah said, "Thank you, Aunt Julia. Would you happen to have an address or telephone number?"

"Sorry, dear. She seems to live quite a solitary life. She doesn't keep in touch with old 'tea' friends."

"Do they have children?" asked Sarah.

"Yes, dear. They have a son called David. I think he lives in London."

Sarah asked after Julia's daughter and her family, thanked Julia again, and disconnected. She bit her lip. India! How would she manage to find Barbara in a country she had never been to and had no connections with? Then she thought of the son, David, who might be in London. She would find him first.

As things sometimes happen, just when she was looking up the name David Preston on the internet, she heard her senior partner, Vera Lyndon, say the name. Her ears pricked up. Vera was telling Logan Mathers, their third partner, something about a David Preston.

Then she called out, "Sarah, this journalist, David Preston, is writing about geriatric care in the UK, and wants to interview one of us. Logan, you look like a movie star, so you'll do justice to the photographs. You are also articulate and charming. So, I propose you. Sarah, could you please second that?"

Sarah hesitated, while Logan asked, "Is he gay?"

Vera sighed and said, "How would I know? I've never met him. How does that matter anyway?"

Logan said, "Well, if he's straight, let him interview our lovely Sarah. Besides, I've done my bit. I lobbied and managed to get some funds for our clinic, didn't I? Fair's fair. I can't be doing all the work."

Vera looked at Sarah with an eyebrow raised in inquiry. "Well?" she asked.

Sarah's pulse was racing but she managed to answer calmly, "I suppose I could do it."

"That's my girl!" said Logan and blew her a kiss as he left the office. Sarah smiled indulgently and Vera sighed, shaking her head.

"So, when am I supposed to meet this journalist?" Sarah asked Vera.

"He'll call Betty and make an appointment," replied Vera, referring to their receptionist.

In the middle of the following week, Betty called Sarah, asking if David Preston could come and meet her at the clinic on Saturday if she was free. Sarah was supposed to go down to Wimbledon for lunch on Saturday, so she told Betty that she'd be able to meet Mr. Preston at 9 AM if that suited him. Betty called her back in a few minutes saying he'd agreed.

Sarah hadn't been able to find out much about David Preston's personal life on the internet. His professional details were available, as he had won a few prestigious journalism awards. Impressive. It looked like he was a "serious" journalist. She just hoped he was Victor and Barbara's son.

Sarah's mouth kept getting dry, and her heart was thumping as it neared 9 AM that Saturday. Vera had suggested she wear something understated but smart. She looked down at her shirt-dress and hoped she'd do. She'd shampooed and blow-dried her chestnut hair. Without false modesty she knew she looked good.

Promptly at 9 AM, Betty ushered in David Preston. He approached her with a friendly smile and shook her hand. He looked around fifty or so, was lean and fit and with a full head of neatly cut salt and pepper hair.

"Thank you for seeing me," he said.

"I hope I didn't disrupt any plans for the weekend," Sarah said apologetically.

"No, not at all," he replied. "I don't usually have plans for 9 AM on a Saturday," he added with a grin.

Sarah smiled, and motioned for him to sit. He sat in an armchair and took out his phone.

"I hope you don't mind if I record our conversation," he said.

"No, that's fine," she said.

For an hour, he asked intelligent and pertinent questions about the standard of geriatric care in the country, and the funds available for it. He asked her for one or two stories about her patients without asking for names. She found him easy to talk to and realized why he was so good at his job. He also asked permission to accompany her on her next visit to Peace Haven. She said she would ask the Administrator and confirm. They exchanged phone numbers, and he started setting up his camera to take a few photographs of her at her desk.

She wondered how to broach the subject of his family. As she was pondering over the best way to bring up the topic, he asked her, "So, have you always lived in London?"

She grabbed the opportunity and replied, "I was born in San Francisco, but came to England when I was three. I lived in Wimbledon till I moved here to study medicine. What about you?"

"I was born in India, and grew up there. In fact, my parents stayed on there, but I came here to study. After completing my Masters in journalism, I got a job straight away, and stayed on."

Sarah's heart was thumping, but she managed to say, "Really? My mother was born in India too!"

David looked at her with interest and said, "What a coincidence!"

"Her father was a tea planter in Assam," added Sarah.

David stared at her. "I can't believe this!" he exclaimed. "Dad was a tea planter in Assam too! Do you know which part of Assam your grandfather was posted in, and the name of the company he worked for?"

Sarah shook her head and said, "No, sorry."

"Where do your grandparents live now?" he asked.

Sarah said, "They're both dead. My grandmother passed away about a month ago, but my grandfather died in India when my mother was four. That's when she and my grandmother returned to England."

"I'm sorry. What about your mother? Would she know any details?" asked David.

"I don't think so. She was too young," replied Sarah quietly.

He asked hesitantly, "Did your grandfather die of a tropical disease in India? Malaria, typhoid, or something like that?"

She shook her head and said, "No. He died in an accident. Actually, I… I… don't know much about it," she hastily added. She didn't want to bring up Harris McIntosh's name, in case he knew that was the name of his mother's ex-husband.

She looked at him and wondered which parent he resembled. Cathy had told Anne that Barbara was beautiful, and that Victor had been very handsome. David was not handsome in the clean-cut way that Logan was, but he was good looking. He was probably about 5 feet 10 inches in height, and had an attractive smile. Behind his glasses, his eyes were blue-grey and crinkled at the corners when he smiled. She thought his good looks were not the obvious kind, but the kind that grew on you.

He said, "Look, if you're free after this, could we go somewhere for a coffee? Or breakfast? I must confess I haven't eaten anything since I woke up!"

She looked at her watch and saw that it was only 10.30 AM, so she had plenty of time to drive down to Wimbledon for lunch.

She said, "Okay, sure. I have to go to my parents' place for a late lunch, but there's plenty of time. And I haven't had breakfast either." She was perfectly happy at the way things were working out. She would have breakfast with him and find out as much as she could about Barbara.

He smiled warmly and said, "Great! I'll just take some photographs, and then we can go. Where would you like to have breakfast?"

She shrugged, saying, "Surprise me."

While they were at breakfast, Mark called, asking if she could get him his favorite Assam tea from Twinings. "Your Gran got me hooked onto that particular tea, and now anything else tastes like horse piss!" he said.

Sarah laughed and said, "Of course, Dad. I'll pick it up. Talking about Assam tea, you won't believe the coincidence! You remember I told you a journalist was interviewing me today for an article on geriatric care? Well, his father was also a tea planter, like my grandfather!"

Mark said, "Wow! Really? That's a coincidence all right! Did they know each other? His father and Oliver, I mean?"

Sarah suddenly went cold, and said, "I don't know, Dad. Gran would have known."

"I suppose your Mum wouldn't remember, but he could ask his parents, couldn't he?" asked Mark.

"Yes, yes, I suppose he could ask his mother. His father passed away a few years ago," said Sarah. But she was not going to suggest it. She didn't want Barbara to be warned. Sarah Sheldon Ainsley couldn't be connected with Oliver Munroe, but Cathy or Anne could.

She disconnected, walked back to the table and said, "Sorry about that. Dad wants me to pick up his favorite brand of tea."

David smiled and said, "No problem."

"So, tell me about your mother. Whereabouts in India does she live?" asked Sarah.

***

On reaching her parents' place, she hugged Mark and Ben who were watching a tennis match on television, companionably discussing the finer points. She took her mother into the garden and sat her down under the colorful sun umbrella.

"Mum," she said. "Do you believe in Fate?"

"I… I haven't really thought about it, Darling. Why do you ask?" asked Anne.

"I've met David Preston," said Sarah.

Her mother wrinkled her brow and asked, "Who? Should I know him?"

"Barbara and Victor's son, Mum," said Sarah.

Her mother's eyes widened, and she whispered, "How? Where?"

Sarah explained how she had met David. Anne asked what he was like, and Sarah had to admit that he was nice.

"I'm going to get to know him, Mum, and find out all I can about Barbara. As I told you on the phone, she lives alone in Shillong. Perhaps you've been there with your parents as a child. Anyway, I need to find out more about her. So, who better to find out from than her own son?"

Anne looked at her daughter and asked, "What are you going to do with the information, Sarah?"

"I don't know yet, Mum. But Barbara Preston was responsible for your father's murder. She made Gran a widow when she was still so young. She may not have meant for that to happen, but her lie led to Oliver's death and she's got off scot-free."

Anne said, "Darling, we don't know that. People suffer for their actions in different ways. Gran said Barbara was a nice person. She didn't know why Barbara had married Harris, because she didn't seem to be in love with him. She was a good and dutiful wife, though, till she met Victor. I suppose they couldn't help falling in love."

"But she should have told Harris the truth," said Sarah uncompromisingly.

"I imagine it wasn't so easy to leave your husband and marry someone in the same social circles those days, Darling. Especially in the tea estates, which is still a close-knit community according to Julia and Mary. Harris was short tempered, and that probably scared Barbara. However, she couldn't have dreamed that Harris would kill my father," said Anne.

"Why are you making excuses for her, Mum?" asked Sarah angrily.

"I'm not making excuses, Darling. Just trying to be fair," said Anne gently. "Please try and keep a sense of proportion. It all happened a long time ago. Long before you were even born. Oliver, your Gran, Harris and Victor are all gone. Poor Harris suffered years of remorse and torment."

"Yes, and who was responsible for that too?" asked Sarah.

Anne took Sarah's hand and said, "Darling, I know you've always had this keen sense of justice and fairness. You couldn't bear for a wrong not to be put right. But life isn't all black and white. And people make mistakes which they might regret forever. I've been giving this a lot of thought. I believe we should let it go. I wish

I hadn't told you, but I had just got to know the truth from Gran, and then she died soon after, and I had to share it with someone."

Sarah said stubbornly, "I can't let it go, Mum. It is just not fair. I need to at least know if Barbara regretted what she did. And, anyway, why did Fate arrange for me to meet David Preston now?"

"I don't know, darling. Perhaps for some other reasons?" answered her mother.

Sarah looked at her mother sharply but Anne stood up and said, "Let's pry those two away from the television and have some lunch."

***

Sarah dialed David's number. She had spoken to Dr Pollard, the Administrator at Peace Haven, who was quite willing to show David around the premises and introduce him to some of the residents. David picked up after a few rings, and said, "Sorry, sorry! I was in the shower." Sarah suddenly had a vision of his lean, naked body in the shower and shook her head to dispel the image.

"I go to Peace Haven on Tuesday and Friday mornings, so when would you like to go?" she asked.

"Oh, great! They've given their permission! Umm… tomorrow's Tuesday, but I'm not free. Friday's fine. Shall I come to your clinic first? What time?" he asked.

Sarah said, "I leave quite early. Where do you live? Perhaps I could pick you up?"

He told her the address which happened to be just around the corner from her place. She couldn't believe it!

"I think it would be faster for me to pick you up. 8.30 AM sharp on Friday, then. See you," she said and rang off.

On Friday morning, she parked the car in front of David's apartment building and called him. But he was already walking out the front door, putting his arm through his coat sleeve. His attractiveness hit her quite hard this time. "Grows on you indeed!" she thought to herself wryly. "That was quick!"

"Good morning," he said, opening the passenger door and settling in. She smiled politely and returned his greeting.

At Peace Haven, she introduced David to Dr Pollard and got on with her rounds. Later, she found him sitting and chatting with a few residents in the recreation room. She watched him listening to them with courteous attention.

She wondered how she would continue meeting him after his article was done. He didn't wear a wedding ring, but he could be in a relationship. She knew he was straight, because the vibes she got from him were pretty heterosexual. She hadn't missed the discreet once-over he had given her the first time they had met and then again that morning as he got into the car.

She had to get closer to him to find out about his mother and eventually get to meet her. She was still a bit vague about what she would do when she did come face to face with Barbara. All she knew was that the woman responsible for getting her grandfather killed, thus depriving her adored Gran of her husband, and her beloved mother of her father, couldn't just go unpunished. Yes, Barbara was an old woman by now. Eighty at least. That didn't matter. One had to face up to one's misdeeds and bear the consequences of one's actions no matter what one's age.

She walked up to David, smiled at the residents and said, "Sorry to intrude, but will you be long, David?"

David said, "No, almost done. I've been regaled with some marvelous stories by these ladies and gentlemen here. I'll just take a few photographs. Won't be long."

"That's fine. I'll be in Dr Pollard's office. You could meet me there once you're done," said Sarah.

As they drove away from Peace Haven, David said, "Thanks for bringing me along. It was such an interesting experience. The residents are well looked after and content. They all like you very much."

Sarah smiled, saying, "I like most of them too."

When Sarah dropped David home, he hesitated then said, "I'll let you know when the article is out. But, if you're free, would you like to have dinner with me tomorrow night?"

Sarah looked at him straight and said, "Yes, I'm free, but are you?"

He instantly understood and said, "Not totally, but in the process. Separated, and getting divorced."

She looked into his eyes which looked back at her openly, without guile. Such beautiful eyes! A little shaken, she said, "All right. Sure. I'd like that."

David exhaled and said, "Good. What kind of cuisine do you like?"

Sarah said, "Let's go for Indian." It seemed appropriate.

"Indian it is," said David. "I'll text you the time and place once I've made the reservations." He waved and watched as she drove away.

Sarah realized she had to get a grip on herself. She could so easily fall in love with David, and that would complicate things. How could she confront his mother and bring her wrongdoing to light if she fell in love with him? Then she smiled wryly, thinking, "As if any of us **chooses** to fall in love, or not, with someone!" She thought of David's parents. They probably hadn't wanted to fall in love with each other. But that wasn't the issue. It was the fact that Barbara had lied without a thought for the consequences, and got Oliver, an innocent man, killed.

Until she fell asleep that night, and then for the whole day until she met David the next evening, she couldn't stop thinking of him. Ironically, one of her schoolfriends posted a message on Facebook which said, "If you can't get somebody off your mind, they are probably supposed to be there."

"Thanks a lot," she thought wryly, "that really helps!"

Over the next fortnight, she and David met four times. He was pleasantly surprised to know that they were practically neighbors. Sarah realized that they never seemed to run out of conversation. Even the short silences were easy. He talked proudly about his son, Vic, who was a conservationist and wildlife filmmaker.

"He's in Shillong at the moment, with my mother. He's making a film about the living root bridges in a place which is an hour's drive from Shillong."

Sarah was intrigued and asked David questions about the bridges.

"They're foot bridges made by entwining the aerial roots of trees," he explained. "Perhaps I can show them to you one day."

Her heart lurched. "Yes, I'd love to see them," she replied, thinking, "Hopefully soon, while your mother's still alive."

She knew she was falling in love with him and there wasn't anything she could do about it. He seemed to be equally smitten, though slightly cautious. She wondered how his wife could bear to let him go, but then he told her that it was his wife who had wanted to end their marriage.

"We were quite young when we married, and although we were physically attracted to each other, we didn't have many interests in common. But we lived together happily enough till a couple of years ago, when Val, my wife, decided that we shouldn't waste our lives just 'chugging along' with each other, as she put it, but call it quits and try and find our real soulmates. A few months ago, she found hers. Funnily enough, he's someone we've both known for years. When I look back, I see how attuned they always were to each other, but they didn't fall in love till now. I suppose what's meant to happen will happen when the time's right. She filed for divorce a couple of months ago, and I'm not contesting it, so the decree should be final in another few months."

"Do you mind?" she asked curiously, adding hastily, "Sorry! That's none of my business."

"No, no, that's fine. I'm very happy for them. I love Val, but I suppose I haven't been 'in love' with her for years," replied David.

Thinking back to this conversation now, Sarah blessed Val for her good sense. At thirty-six, she had more or less given up the idea of finding the "right man" but here he was! And here **she** was, planning on confronting his mother and bringing her to book! Although she still didn't know how. Being a geriatrician, her conscience smote her. "I am supposed to care for the elderly!" she thought. Her phone rang, jerking her out of her reverie. It was David.

"Sarah, listen. I just heard from Vic. I have to go and see my mother. She's… she's not well," he said. "I hate to leave you just when we're getting to know each other, but I really need to go."

Sarah's mind was racing. She was due some leave. This might be the perfect opportunity to confront Barbara. "She's not well," thought the geriatrician in her sympathetically, but then she thought of her murdered grandfather and hardened her heart.

"I'm sorry to hear that your mother's not well, David." Then she took a deep breath and asked, "Would you like to take a geriatrician along with you?"

She heard David's sharp intake of breath. "Really? You'd go with me?" he asked with a tenderness she hadn't heard before.

Her conscience smote her again, but she said steadily, "Yes. I have some leave pending. Besides, once your mother's better, you can take me to see those bridges."

"That's a promise!" he said, and added, "Sarah, thank you, but I need to leave within the next week. Is that too soon for you?"

"Umm… I think I can manage that," she said confidently, but with fingers crossed.

"Is your passport valid for the next six months? You could apply for a visa online. It takes about two to four days. My visa is still valid, so as soon as you get yours, I'll get our tickets," said David. "Let me know how many days' leave you can take."

Sarah said, "Yes, my passport is valid for the next five years, actually. I'll speak to Vera and Logan, apply for my visa, and get back to you, so that we can do our tickets on the same flight."

David said, "I thought I'd do them together so that I can book our seats next to each other."

Sarah said, "Umm, okay. Let me know the fare so that I can transfer you the money." David said he'd do that, and disconnected.

Logan scowled at her mock ferociously saying he couldn't possibly look after her patients while she was away, but finally laughed, gave her a hug and said, "Away, woman. It's time you took a few days off."

Vera told her to enjoy her well-deserved holiday too.

Sarah had many last-minute things to organize at work in the next few days, so she didn't have time to visit her parents before her trip. When she called to say goodbye, Anne was full of misgivings.

"Sarah, please don't do anything foolish and get yourself into trouble," she said in a worried tone. "It all happened such a long time ago. Will you please just let it go?"

"Mum, I look after elderly people. This woman is sick. What do you think I'm going to do to her?" asked Sarah. But as she said the words, she wondered if she **would** contemplate harming the woman if she had to. She didn't know what to expect, but she was prepared for anything. "Just let her show some remorse, please," she prayed silently. "Let her admit her culpability and show remorse." Then Sarah would get closure for Anne and Cathy, and her grandfather could rest in peace. But if Barbara didn't admit to anything, what was she, Sarah, going to do? How far was she willing to go to avenge her family, and lose David in the process? She didn't know the answer.

Sarah looked down at the forested hills and the river Brahmaputra meandering beneath them as the plane started its descent into Guwahati airport. Once they collected their luggage, they walked out and Sarah saw a young man resembling David waving at them. David called, "Vic!" and rushed up to hug him.

Vic shook hands with Sarah and said, "Pleased to meet you."

He led them to the hired car and introduced them to the driver, who placed their luggage in the trunk. Vic sat beside the driver in front while David and Sarah sat behind. The two-hour drive up to Shillong was through verdant hills, and they rolled the windows down to let the cool, pine-scented breeze waft in. They stopped for tea and snacks midway, at a place called Nongpoh, and then again at the scenic Umiam lake to take photographs. David placed his arm around her shoulders, pulling her close, and she thought how right that felt. Although he was worried about his mother, he seemed relaxed and happy.

As they got closer to Shillong, Sarah started getting butterflies in her stomach. She would soon be face to face with Barbara. What would she say or do? What would happen to David and her relationship once he knew the truth? She glanced at him as he spoke to Vic. He felt her look and turned to smile at her, reaching out to hold her hand. He was much more demonstrative here, for some reason. She found it endearing. She managed a smile, then turned and looked out of the window, feeling sick at heart. Having found this precious man, how could she bear to lose him?

They entered the town and drove to Upper Shillong, the area where Victor had built a charming two-story cottage and named it "Endeavour." The gate was open, and they drove into a pretty garden with a profusion of flowers. Sarah was feeling so sick that she thought she might throw up. David looked at her pale face with concern.

"Are you all right, Love?" he asked. It was the very first time he had called her that, or used any term of endearment, she realized with a pang. She nodded, but he told Vic, "I think the journey's got to her. Can you take the luggage in? Hers is the maroon suitcase." Vic picked it up and was turning into David's room when his father called out, "You can take it up to the guestroom." Vic raised an eyebrow in surprise, but did as he was told. Two middle-aged women were waiting at the door to welcome them warmly in broken English. David introduced them to Sarah who managed to smile weakly at them.

David held her around the waist and led her gently up the wooden staircase to the guestroom. "The bathroom's attached. Just freshen up and rest. I'll bring you some hot, sweet tea." Sarah's stomach heaved but she just nodded again. "My poor darling," said David, kissing her forehead gently. Sarah almost burst into tears.

Love! Darling! Kisses! What a time he'd chosen to be so loving! Just when she had to confront his mother – the woman responsible for her grandfather's death – and renounce her, or whatever! How unfair life was!

David took the bedcover off, asked if she would be all right, then left the room as Sarah went into the bathroom. There, she was violently sick. She cleaned up and washed her face, then she walked shakily back into the room, lay on the bed and fell asleep.

When she woke up, the bedside lamp was on, and there was a tray with a covered pot of tea, a cup and saucer, milk pot, sugar bowl, and a plate of biscuits, on the table between two armchairs. She swung her legs off the bed and sat still for a moment. She looked at the clock on the wall. Its hands stood at 6 o'clock. So, it was 6 PM. She had slept for an hour. She went to the bathroom and washed her face, then walked to the armchair and sat down. She poured herself a cup of tea and had a biscuit. Her stomach had settled and she was a little peckish.

At the thought of her imminent meeting with Barbara, however, the butterflies started an uproar in her stomach again. There was a gentle knock on her door, and then it opened and David popped his head in. "Feeling better?" he asked.

Sarah nodded and asked, "How's your mother?"

David entered the room and sat on the other armchair. He frowned and said, "She's worse than when I last met her." Before she could ask what was wrong, he said, "But you can come and meet her if you're feeling up to it."

Much as Sarah wanted to say she wasn't feeling up to it, she knew she couldn't avoid meeting Barbara. That's what she had come for, after all. She finished her tea, and stood up. David stood too, and put his arms around her. He looked into her eyes and kissed her deeply. She kissed him back with all her heart, thinking, "This could well be our last kiss." He pulled away reluctantly and led her out. Heart hammering for more than one reason, Sarah followed him on leaden feet.

They entered the drawing room and David said, "Mum, I've brought you a visitor." The old lady sitting on the sofa next to Vic looked at David and smiled sweetly, but without recognition. He said, "This is Sarah. She's come all the way from England to see you." Barbara smiled again.

"She doesn't recognize me," said David sadly. "She did the last time I was here six months ago. She doesn't say much either. Vic says she has moments of lucidity, but they're few and far between."

As Sarah stared into the vacant eyes of the still beautiful woman, she recognized the signs of dementia. Barbara didn't know her own son, so what would she remember of events that had taken place so long ago, and the people of that time?

Sarah asked David, "Who looks after her?"

"The two women you met - Kong Drien and Kong Plina. We address them as 'Kong' which means 'elder sister' in the local Khasi language. They have been her loyal companions and lived and worked in this house since Dad retired and moved here with Mum," said David. "Would you check her up thoroughly tomorrow? The local doctor told Vic that her heart is enlarged and her kidneys aren't functioning too well."

Sarah nodded, saying, "Of course. Perhaps I could talk to her doctor too."

David nodded and said, "Vic wants to discuss something with me. I've given the Kongs some time off this evening. Could I ask you to sit with Mum for a while, if you don't mind?"

Sarah said, "No, I don't mind at all."

David squeezed her shoulder, then left the room with Vic, who gave her a warm smile as he walked out.

Sarah stared at Barbara. She was actually alone with the woman who had caused her grandfather's murder! How ironic that the woman couldn't remember anything about it, or the part she had played in the tragedy. Or could she?

Sarah said loudly, "Harris!" At the sound of her voice, Barbara turned to look at her, but there was no other reaction. "Oliver," said Sarah. Barbara looked at her blankly. Then she smiled that sweet, vacant smile again, and turned away.

Sarah stared at Barbara and slowly, something shifted inside her and the animosity fell away. Barbara was the only one besides Harris who had known, or at least suspected, that Oliver's death had been no accident. She had caused his death as surely if she had pulled the trigger. It must have been traumatic for her, a basically decent woman. Sarah thought of the years and years that this woman had carried her guilt within her. She must not have told even Victor, out of fear that he would be repulsed, and leave her. He might have insisted on telling the police too. How lonely it must have been to carry such a secret alone, and for so long! Perhaps, in the end, she couldn't deal with that truth, and had let go of her mind rather than remember that she had caused one man's death and the destruction of another man's soul. It was like suffering from Post-Traumatic Stress Disorder, which was known to cause dementia.

Sarah remembered her mother's words about people paying for their sins in different ways, and was overcome with pity, and yes, compassion for Barbara. She may not have been punished by society, but she had paid a heavy price. Sarah suddenly remembered a quotation she had read somewhere – "the greatest revenge is compassion," and realized wryly that she had got her revenge.

***

David knocked on her door that night, poked his head in, and looked at her enquiringly. She sat up, and smiled lovingly at him. He shut the door softly and climbed into bed with her. As he held her and smiled into her eyes, she felt her own eyes welling with tears. Just a few hours ago, she had thought she might lose him forever.

"What's wrong, Darling?" he asked tenderly.

"Nothing!" she exclaimed. "I'm just so happy!" She squeezed him so tight, that he grunted and gasped, "Easy, Love. I can't breathe!"

She loosened her hold and whispered, "I love you," reveling in the freedom to tell him that at last.

***

In her bedroom downstairs, Barbara gazed unseeingly out of the window as Kong Plina got her room ready for the night. Slowly, as the clouds parted to let the full moon shine bright, the mist in her mind also lifted for a moment and a lovely face framed in chestnut hair that she knew from decades ago, but vaguely sensed she had seen recently, appeared before her eyes. "Cathy?" she whispered.

And her worn heart gave an agonized leap.

The Long Shadow

Old sins cast long shadows. (Proverb)

JULIE – 2016

Julie entered her mother's bedroom and sat on the window seat opposite the bed. She looked around the familiar room and then stared out of the window at the distant pine-covered hills. How her mother had loved the smell of the pine needles! Julie had so many memories of walks in the pine woods with her mother over the years. They would walk in companionable silence, stopping to collect dry pine needles, twigs, and pine cones for the fire place. Tears welled in her eyes but she quickly dabbed at them with her handkerchief when she heard her husband calling out to her.

"Coming!" she called, and taking another look around the room, walked out.

They had returned from the cemetery a couple of hours ago, after burying Julie's mother. Norah Lyngdoh had been a nurse for most of her life and was universally loved in her neighborhood. Kong Norah, as she had been respectfully called by everyone who knew her, had always been ready to help people in any way she could. As Julie shook hands and accepted the condolences of her mother's friends and neighbors, she was overwhelmed by the number of people who had turned up to pay their last respects to her mother. She knew some of them but many were strangers.

When the last visitor had left, Julie sat wearily down on the sofa and put her aching feet on the footstool. Looking at her mother's photograph on the piano, she sighed while tears filled her eyes. Her husband, Arup, sat beside her and put his arm around her shoulders in silent sympathy. She leaned her head on his shoulder gratefully and closed her eyes. Arup looked at her tenderly and even after thirty years of marriage, his breath caught in his throat at the sheer loveliness of her. They stayed that way till Julie's uncle, Peter, placed his hand gently on Arup's shoulder and handed him a letter. Arup glanced at the letter addressed to Julie in Norah's handwriting, and raised his eyebrows in query.

Peter shrugged and said quietly, "My sister asked me to give this letter to Julie after her death. That's all I know."

Arup thanked him and placed the letter on the center table. He looked at the photograph of his late mother-in-law and remembered her affection and kindness towards him. It had not mattered to her that he was not from the same community or religion. She was happy that he respected theirs and even went to church with her and Julie on Sundays when they were staying with her.

He thought of the impromptu "sing-songs" (as Norah liked to call them) around the piano. She played beautifully, and Julie had a true voice. Peter played the guitar and he, his wife Dora, and Arup himself were all good singers.

"We didn't do too badly, really," he thought fondly, smiling at the memories, specially of Christmas, which had always been a special occasion.

But much as he had respected and loved his mother-in-law, he always felt that she kept a little of herself away even from Julie. He looked at the letter on the table and wondered what it said.

Julie stirred and woke up. She looked up at Arup and smiled lovingly. He smiled back and tightened his arm around her shoulders. Then he picked up the letter and handed it to her.

"What's this?" she asked and then recognized her mother's handwriting. Her hand trembled as she gazed at the envelope. "Where did this come from?" she asked.

"Uncle Peter gave it to me when he saw that you were sleeping. Mei asked him to give it to you after..." said Arup, unable to say the rest of the words. "Would you like to read it now?"

"Yes... no... I don't know," replied Julie, sounding nervous.

Arup watched her quietly for a while, then asked gently, "Should I unseal the envelope for you?"

"Yes please," whispered Julie.

For some reason, she was reluctant to read the letter. She watched as Arup unsealed the flap and taking out the folded letter, handed it to her. She took it slowly and unfolded it. Arup watched as she read the letter once, and then again, her hand shaking. She handed it to him wordlessly, her face pale and shocked. Arup read the letter quickly and looked at her. They stared at each other in stupefaction.

"Did you ever guess any of this?" Arup asked when he had recovered somewhat.

"No, never!" said Julie. "I know I have brown hair and hazel eyes, but Mei herself had dark brown hair and light eyes, so I never thought about it twice! She told me my father, Harish Das, had died before I was born, and unfortunately, there were no photographs of him. She had met and married him when she was studying Nursing in Guwahati, and he had died soon after they were married and she was expecting me. His parents had disapproved of their marriage and disowned him so we had no connection with them. I didn't think twice about my using **her** surname because that's what is commonly done in our matriarchal society, as you know. Now, I find I'm illegitimate and my father was a British tea planter in Assam! She knew his name and that his family had a farm in England, but nothing else. Ralph Smith! There must be thousands of Ralph Smiths in England! And, obviously, Harish Das never existed!"

Arup looked at her sympathetically and took her hand in his. "Don't think badly of her, Darling. Those times were different. Knowing Mei, she must have loved him deeply and been very hurt when they parted. It must have been pretty difficult for her but your grandparents were supportive. A good thing about your matriarchal society is that people didn't judge unmarried mothers harshly, nor babies born out of wedlock, even in your mother's time. Your grandparents loved you very much too."

"Yes, they did," agreed Julie fondly. "Do you think this Ralph... my father... this man... left Mei because she came from a different class?"

Arup shrugged, saying, "I don't know, Love. Maybe. It mattered in those days. If British planters married local women, their social standing and careers were affected. Perhaps his family would have disowned him too. He was young, and perhaps he didn't have the courage to go against society, the Company, or his family."

Julie looked down at the letter and said softly, "Poor Mei."

"Yes," said Arup softly. Then he lifted her chin gently, looked into her eyes and asked, "This illegitimacy thing doesn't bother you, does it? It shouldn't. It's of no importance whatsoever. No one else needs know about it anyway."

"What about Robin and Maya?" asked Julie.

Arup said thoughtfully, "Well, it does affect them, so they'll have to know. But there's no hurry. I'm sure you need time to take it all in. Tell them when you're ready."

Julie squeezed his hand gratefully and said, "What would I do without you?"

Arup kissed her hand and said, "Come on, let's have some dinner and go to sleep, Love. It's been an emotional day for you." He helped her up and they left the room together.

After locking up her mother's cottage (Julie couldn't get used to its now being hers) Julie and Arup drove back to the tea estate.

Sitting in her favorite armchair by the bedroom fireplace, she read the letter for the umpteenth time. How could her mother have kept this secret from her for all these years? Had she thought that Julie would judge her or mind that she was illegitimate?

"Oh Mei, why did you carry this burden alone for so long?" she asked silently.

She wondered what her father had been like. Was he alive or dead? If he was alive, did she want to meet him? Her heart thudded at the thought. "He must have married and had children. I wonder if he had loved Mei or just been lonely. Or was he a cad? Do I even want to find out?" Her mind was in a whirl.

She thought of her son, Robin, who worked for Microsoft in Seattle, and her daughter, Maya, studying Economics at the

London School of Economics. How would they feel when they came to know that their mother was illegitimate?

"Probably just take it in their stride, knowing those two," thought Julie. "Their generation is so much more non-judgmental of things like this. What will probably intrigue them more is the fact that their grandfather was English."

She suddenly wondered if Maya, being in England, could look for him. Then she shied away from the thought. Why go looking for someone who had left without a word of explanation, never got in touch in all these years, and obviously wouldn't want to be found, especially by a daughter he didn't know existed?

DEREK – 2016

Derek parked the car in the visitors' parking lot, locked it, and walked up the stairs to his parents' condo. His mother opened the door as soon as he rang the bell, and gave him a tight hug.

He kissed her, saying, "You're looking as lovely as ever, Mom." It was true. She had always had this aura of calmness and serenity which added to her natural beauty. She was the most peaceful person he knew. She smiled at the compliment and led him out to the balcony which overlooked the woods beyond which flowed the Sammamish River. His father sat there, holding a pair of binoculars to his eyes, watching the birds and hares sunning themselves on the patch of grass bordering the woods. When he heard the screen door open, he turned and smiled at Derek.

"Hello, dear boy," he said, shaking hands. Derek smiled fondly and put his arms around his father. Even after half a century in USA, his father was still very British. He sat down and asked, "So, what did you want to tell me, Dad?"

Ralph hesitated, and looked at his wife for help. Hallie nodded encouragingly, and said, "I'll leave you boys to talk while I finish cooking lunch."

Derek waited patiently for his father to speak. Being a psychiatrist had its advantages, thought Derek. You had to have patience and good listening skills.

"Good thing I inherited these traits from Mom," thought Derek.

Ralph cleared his throat a couple of times, then said quietly, "A few days ago, I had this memory of a girl I knew back in India. Before the attack."

Derek sat up straight, exclaiming, "Dad! You're getting your memories of that lost time back!"

Ralph nodded, saying, "Yes, it looks like I am. You know I lost my memory after the attack on the tea estate. I couldn't remember anything that had happened for a period before I got hit on the head so brutally. Thankfully, it wasn't worse. The doctors in Calcutta, and later, in London, worked wonders. My brain healed and I didn't have trouble remembering things that happened after that. I had joined the tea company straight after school, so after returning to England, once I knew I couldn't go back to India, I went to college. After graduating from college, I met your mother while we were both holidaying in Italy, as you know. Then I followed her to Seattle, got a job here, married her, and the rest, as they say, is History."

Derek smiled and nodded, then asked curiously, "So, who was this girl in India?"

Ralph stared unseeingly at the woods and said, "She was a student nurse at the hospital I was admitted into when I had a very bad bout of malaria. This was just before the attack. Her name was Norah. I...I fell in love with her. I was twenty-two. She was probably a year younger. I wanted our relationship to develop though she was convinced it wouldn't work, because of class barriers. Those were societal concerns back then, but I had every intention of pursuing the relationship. Then the attack happened, and before I knew it, I was sent back to England for good. And, of course, I had no memory of her. Till now." He turned to look at Derek with tears in his eyes. "God knows what she thought of me. You see, the last time we met, I...we made love. Which was a very big deal back then. Then to not hear from me at all...she must have thought I was a cad of the worst kind. It distresses me to think of what she must have gone through. She was a good person, and she trusted me. I just want to apologize and explain, and know that she's all right. But I have no idea how to get in touch with her now. Where do I even start?”

“Does Mom know all this?” asked Derek.

“Of course!” replied Ralph. “She understands how bad I feel about just leaving the poor girl without a word of explanation.”

“It wasn’t your fault, Dad,” said Derek consolingly.

“I know,” said Ralph, “But that doesn’t make me feel any better. I just keep thinking of the poor girl wondering why I hadn’t returned as promised, nor sent her word of any kind. If only I had told Timothy, my friend and colleague at the estate, about her, he may have thought of telling her what had happened to me. They were both from Shillong, so he may have known her. In fact, they shared the same surname, so he may have even been related to her!”

He covered his eyes with his hands and said in a voice choked with emotion, “I can’t bear to think of the hurt and distress she must have felt.”

NORAH – 1959

Norah looked at the unconscious man on the bed. He had been brought in four days ago with very high fever and convulsions.

“Malaria,” Dr Jones had pronounced and given directions for his treatment.

"Poor boy, he looks so young and helpless," one of the nurses had murmured. According to his records, his name was Ralph Smith and he was twenty-two years old.

"A tea planter from an estate near Silchar," said Sister Randall.

Norah picked up his wrist to feel his pulse. His fever had come down and he seemed to be sleeping peacefully. Suddenly he opened his eyes and looked at her.

She smiled reassuringly but he looked around the unfamiliar room and tried to sit up, asking "Where am I? What am I doing here? Who are you?" Before she could reply, he looked at her uniform and said, "You're a nurse so this is a hospital. Why am I here? Do you speak English?"

"Yes, I speak English," replied Norah, who had been taught by Irish nuns at a convent school in Shillong, the capital town of the state of Assam.

"This is the Satribari Christian Hospital in Gauhati. You were brought here four days ago, unconscious, with very high fever. You had malaria. Dr Jones treated you and now you are better."

"Oh," said the young man thoughtfully.

"I'll just tell Sister that you are conscious. She can answer any other questions you may have," she said and turned to leave.

"Wait, why can't you answer my questions?" he asked.

"I'm a student nurse," replied Norah. "I just check the patient's temperature and pulse."

"Oh," he said again. "But you'll come back, won't you?"

"I have to check on the other patients, but I can come back once I'm done," she replied and smiled in what she hoped was a motherly manner. She could feel his anxious eyes on her as she walked to the door.

When Norah returned as promised sometime later, he was sleeping again. She checked that there was enough water in his jug and gently smoothed the bedsheet covering him. He opened his eyes and smiled at her. Even in his weakened state, the smile was radiant. Norah blinked and tried to still her suddenly racing heart.

"Hello," he said.

"Hello," replied Norah.

"So, you kept your promise and came back," he said.

"Yes," she replied simply.

"My name's Ralph," he said. "What's yours?"

"Norah," she replied.

"It's nice to meet you, Norah, although I would've wished for better circumstances. It's very awkward lying on this bed and looking up at you."

Was he flirting with her? Norah felt flustered and looked around nervously in case Sister was somewhere around.

"I had better go now. My duty is over and I have to do my homework," she said.

"Homework?" he asked.

"Yes. I told you I was a student nurse. This is a teaching hospital. I'm in my final year and my exams are in a month's time."

"Oh, yes. I forgot. When will you be back on duty?" he asked.

"Tomorrow morning, at 6 o'clock. After that I have my classes."

"I'll see you tomorrow, then," he said, with another radiant smile.

"Good night," she mumbled and beat a hasty retreat.

She saw him every morning. He tried to hold her back, talking about his life on the tea estate, and his home on a farm back in England, but she was scared that Sister would find her in his room and get very angry. So, she took his temperature and checked his pulse, duly noted them down and left to check on the next patient. But she always returned to his room to say "goodbye" before going to class. He was like a magnet and she had to fight herself to not linger in his room.

"What is wrong with me?" she asked herself. "He's an Englishman. An executive in a tea company. He's from a different social class altogether. We can't even be friends let alone anything else. Once he leaves, I'll never see him again. He doesn't feel anything for me. He's just bored and lonely." Her eyes filled with tears of hopelessness.

It was his last day. As soon as she entered his room, he took her into his arms.

"Norah, Norah, I'm going to miss you. When will we meet again? Will you write to me?"

She stayed still in his arms and replied, "No. This will have to be goodbye, Ralph."

"Why?" he cried, pulling away to look at her.

"Because we might as well be from different planets," she replied sadly.

"What do you mean?" he asked.

"You are an executive in a tea company. Your family owns a farm. I'm a nurse, or at least will be one soon. My parents are humble people. My father is a carpenter and my mother works as a children's nanny."

"So what? They are respectable people and you are in a respectable profession."

"So, what do you want Ralph? Do you want to be friends? Is that it? Just friends?"

"I... don't know, Norah. All I know is that I don't want to leave you."

Norah looked at him sadly. "I have to go now, Ralph, so I'll say goodbye. God bless you."

She held out her hand. He took it in his and said, "I'm staying at a guest house tonight and leaving early tomorrow morning for Silchar. Will you come and have dinner with me, please? At least we can meet one last time and say a proper goodbye."

Norah hesitated, but the thought of spending some time with him away from the hospital was too tempting.

"Please, Norah. At least we can spend some time together properly instead of your looking over your shoulder all the time and running away at the first hint of a footstep!"

Later, she thought she should have known what would happen. The evening was charged with emotion, and being alone together was too heady a freedom for them both. Before she knew what was happening, they were on the bed with their clothes off. She had never imagined that she could feel so much love for a person. She gave of herself generously, as did he. Inexperienced they both might have been, but they came together as if they were made for each other. At the last minute, Ralph quickly rolled away, mumbling, "I don't want to get you into trouble."

He looked at her to see if she understood. She nodded shyly. He held her tenderly, kissing her hair and face over and over again. She kissed him back with all her heart. She stole glances at his body and thought that she had never seen anything more beautiful. When he smiled teasingly and asked, "Do you like what you see?" She nodded and told him what she was thinking. He exclaimed in a moved tone, "Sweetheart, it's you who are beautiful. So beautiful!"

The next day, Ralph went back to the estate, promising to return a fortnight later, but that was the last she had seen of him. When she found she was pregnant, she asked to see the patients' register for Ralph's address, or at least the name of his estate. After a great deal of hesitation, she wrote to him telling him of her pregnancy. He never replied. She didn't even know if he had received her letter, the postal service being what it was in those days, especially in remote areas such as the tea estate at which he was posted.

Fortunately, her final examinations were over, and she could go home to Shillong. Although her heart quailed at the thought of telling her parents about her pregnancy, she longed for the comfort of their presence and of being back home.

To her great relief, her parents took the news quite calmly, and were very supportive. "We know our daughter, my dear," said her mother. "You must love the man very much."

Norah nodded miserably, and told them all that had transpired. She said, "I was the one who didn't think we had a future together, but he did. I know he was sincere. I just don't understand what happened to make him change his mind."

Her father, a devout man, said, "Let us not judge him, my dear, until we know the circumstances."

Her mother nodded, saying, "We don't know why he didn't come back to see you, or reply to your letter, or even if he got the letter. Let's wait and see if he gets in touch. He can get your address from the hospital."

Norah's parents loved Julie from the moment she was born, and looked after her happily when Norah started working at a local hospital. Norah's mother had retired, and her father had two other carpenters working under him, so he had some free time, although he still obliged his old customers with carpentry work that they didn't want to entrust to anyone else.

Over the years, although Ralph's memory and the pain of loss slowly faded, Norah didn't meet anyone else she wanted to marry. She was content with her work at the hospital, and with her life at home with her parents and Julie. Her experience with Ralph did not make her bitter. Instead, it made her kinder, and more empathetic and compassionate.

When Julie asked about her father, Norah told her that he had died soon after Julie was born. Since his parents had disapproved of their marriage, she didn't have any communication with them. Norah thought vaguely that perhaps one day, when the time was right, she would tell Julie the truth, but the years passed, and somehow, the right moment never presented itself.

RALPH – 1959

Ralph bumped his way back to his estate on the badly maintained roads full of potholes. Timothy, his colleague who was driving, turned and grinned at him every time Ralph almost flew off his seat.

"Hey, slow down, Tim!" he shouted. "I've lost so much weight that even gravity can't hold me down on my seat!"

Timothy grinned, saying, "Now that you mention it Ralph, you **do** look like a scarecrow!"

"Thanks a lot, Timothy!" said Ralph dryly.

"Actually, you look quite good for someone who's just recovered from malaria. You also look remarkably happy. Did you take a fancy to one of the nurses?" asked Timothy slyly.

Ralph stole a quick glance at Timothy, and drawled, "Oh yeah, sure. With Sister, the Dragon Lady, breathing down their necks, they have all the time in the world to fraternize with patients!"

Timothy grinned appreciatively, but turned serious and said, "We should get back to the estate before sunset. There have been a series of robberies in our neighboring estates. A gang of men armed with knives have entered bungalows, overpowered the *chowkidar* and robbed the residents. Luckily, no one has been injured, or worse, so far. But we're all taking precautions. Every bungalow has two *chowkidars* at night now."

"That's alarming news. What are the police doing?" asked Ralph. "Do they have any information about the gang?"

"They're gathering information, but have asked us to take our own precautions till they nab the gang," replied Timothy.

It was two nights later that the gang of thieves entered Ralph's bungalow and overpowered one *chowkidar*. The other had enough time to run out and bang on the gong before he too was overpowered. The gang would have probably run off before the workers responded to the gong, which signaled distress, had Ralph not unthinkingly reacted and come out of his room. Shouting, he charged at them, and one of the gang picked up a brass fire iron and hit him hard on the head. As Ralph fell unconscious, the gang made their escape just as the first workers appeared in response to the gong.

The estate's doctor said gravely that Ralph had to be airlifted to Gauhati airport and taken straight to Calcutta for treatment. An army helicopter took him to Gauhati airport, from where he was flown to Calcutta, and straight to a well-known hospital for treatment. A blood clot had formed in his brain, so a hole had to be drilled in his skull to drain out the blood and release the pressure on his brain. Once he was stable, he was flown to London at the company's expense, and treated at a hospital which specialized in brain injuries. His mother stayed at her sister's flat in London and spent most of her time in the hospital with Ralph. His worried father tried to come on weekends but had too much work at the farm, all of which he couldn't leave to Ralph's older brother, Graham, so he contented himself with daily bulletins on Ralph's progress.

Once Ralph was pronounced fit enough to travel, he and his mother took the train back to the farm up in Surrey.

There was no question of Ralph's going back to India, so he helped on the farm while he decided what to do with his life.

Although he was fully recovered, he had no memories of the period immediately before and after the attack. This bothered him but the doctor said it was better not to force the issue.

"Perhaps it's better to forget the traumatic event anyway, eh?" the doctor said.

But Ralph had the feeling that he had forgotten something important. He wondered if he would ever get those memories back. The doctor hadn't been able to reassure him.

"The brain is such a delicate and unpredictable organ. Just be happy you've recovered fully, my boy. Losing a few memories is nothing compared to what else you could have lost. Believe me, it could've been so much worse."

Ralph knew the doctor was right. He got such a terrible headache when he tried to remember, that he let it go, though he couldn't get over the feeling that there was something important he should remember.

DEREK – 2016

As Derek drove back to his clinic in Bellevue from his parents' place in Kenmore, he mulled over what his father had told him. He understood how troubled Ralph was about having let Norah down, however unintentionally. He wanted to help but had no idea where to start. Unfortunately, his father couldn't remember the name of the hospital in Gauhati where he had been admitted. After he had returned to England, he hadn't kept in touch with Timothy or any of his other friends in India. Derek understood how difficult communications between people in different countries must have been in the 1960s. Airmail letters took ages to reach their destination. "Thank goodness we have mobile phones and email now," he thought.

When he got home that evening, his wife, Susan, kissed him, and with her arms around his neck, asked, "So, what was the urgent issue your Dad wanted to discuss with you?" He kissed the top of her head and led her to the sofa. Sitting with his arm around her shoulders, he told her how Ralph had suddenly got back his lost memories, and about his short-lived love affair with Norah.

"He feels so guilty about the way he left her without a word of explanation, although it wasn't his fault. I hate to see him so distressed, Sue. I wish I could help him."

Susan squeezed his hand sympathetically, but sat lost in thought for a while. Then she suddenly exclaimed, "I know why the name Shillong seems familiar!"

When Derek looked at her enquiringly, Susan continued, "Do you remember my telling you about the boy from India who's on my team? Robin Baruah? Whose father is a tea planter from Assam? I was excited because of the coincidence. You know, since your Dad was also a tea planter in Assam for a few years."

Derek nodded, saying, "Yes, I remember you mentioning his name and the fact that his father is a tea planter in Assam."

Susan teased, saying, "Ah, so you do listen to me, Doctor. Sometimes I wonder if you tune out when I talk to you. Although I wouldn't blame you if you did, after spending hours listening to other people's problems."

Derek squeezed her shoulders hard and said, "Take that back! You know I always listen to you. In fact, I'm putty in your hands!" Then he asked seriously, "But what's the connection between this guy and Shillong?"

"Well, he went to school in Shillong. I remember the name from his resume because I found it so similar to 'shilling.' You know, your Dad would tell us how something cost this many shillings and that many pence when he was a child in England."

Derek nodded. Then he said, "I wonder if he knows Norah, or knows someone who knows her. I know it's a long shot, but coincidences do happen, and he's the only connection we have to Norah's hometown. Will you ask him, please? Her name is Norah Lyngdoh."

He spelt the name out for her, so that Susan could note it down on her phone.

The next day, Derek got a message from Susan asking him what time he would be home that evening. When he replied that he would be back by 6 PM, she mentioned that she would be bringing someone home for him to meet. Derek immediately knew it was Robin.

"He must know Norah, or of her," he thought, and felt a frisson of excitement. He somehow got through the day and the ten-minute drive back home suddenly seemed never-ending!

As Derek entered the living room from the garage, the young man sitting in one of the armchairs stood up respectfully and said "Good evening, Sir."

Derek returned his greeting and Susan introduced them saying, "Derek, this is my colleague Robin Baruah. Robin, my husband, Derek."

The men shook hands, and Derek said, "Please, do sit down."

Robin thanked him and sat in the armchair while Derek sat on the sofa next to Susan. Derek looked from Susan to Robin, and asked, "I don't mean to be abrupt, but I'm guessing you have something to tell me about Norah Lyngdoh. Do you know her?"

Robin said softly, "She was my grandmother."

Derek was staggered. He looked at Robin and said faintly, "I certainly hadn't expected that!"

Susan squeezed his hand gently and said, "Robin lived with his grandmother while he was at school. He was very close to her. Unfortunately, she died a few months ago."

"Oh, I'm so sorry for your loss," said Derek sincerely.

Robin thanked him with a quiet dignity and said, "She was a wonderful person. I thought the world of her. She was kind and compassionate. That's why she was such a great nurse."

Derek and Susan nodded in understanding. "I'm guessing she was your mother's mother," said Derek.

"Yes, that's right," said Robin. "My mother, Julie, is her only child."

Derek stared at Robin, thinking there was an elusive familiarity in the boy's features that he couldn't quite put his finger on. He asked, "What about your grandfather? Your mother's father?"

Robin looked at Susan.

"Please tell Derek what you told me about your grandfather, Robin," she said encouragingly. "Believe me, it's important."

Derek shot Susan a glance, and Robin looked a bit puzzled, but cleared his throat and said, "We got to know this only after Granny died, when her brother Peter gave Mum a letter Granny had written to her. She had always told Mum that her father had died before she was born. She didn't have any photographs of him, and wasn't in contact with his family because they had refused to acknowledge her. Mum believed her and stopped asking questions. But in that letter, Granny wrote that Mum's father was a British tea planter called Ralph Smith. They had been in love but he never came back to meet her as he'd promised, nor acknowledged her letter saying she was pregnant."

He looked from Derek to Susan uncertainly and said, "I'm not sure why Susan wanted me to tell you this, Sir. I mean, I know you wanted to contact Granny for some reason, but I don't see how all this could be relevant to you."

Derek felt the small hairs at the back of his neck rise. Whatever he had expected, it wasn't this! Yes, he believed in coincidences, but a coincidence of this magnitude! This revelation was absolutely staggering! When he saw two pairs of eyes rivetted on him, he realized he hadn't said a word.

He roused himself and asked Susan, "So, you didn't tell him about Dad?"

Susan shook her head, saying, "No, I thought you should tell him."

Derek took a deep breath and said, "Well Robin, my father is an Englishman called Ralph Smith. He was a tea planter in Assam for a few years in the late 1950s."

Robin's eyes widened as he took that in. He stammered as he said, "But…but I thought your surname was Mallory!"

Susan said, "That's my maiden name. I've kept that for professional purposes because it's on all my certificates. Derek's surname is Smith."

Robin looked just as poleaxed as Derek felt. They stared at each other in silence.

Then Robin flushed and stammered out, "I'd…I'd like to know why your father treated my grandmother so badly, Sir. She didn't deserve to be treated like that."

Derek said, "Please, call me Derek." Then he told Robin what had happened to Ralph and why he hadn't been able to get in touch with Norah all these years.

"He only very recently remembered her, and is feeling so wretched about how he must have hurt her."

Robin mulled the information over, and said slowly, "It wasn't his fault." Then he added, "I'm glad he recovered from that awful attack."

They looked at each other in silence again until Derek said, "You do realize he's your grandfather and I'm your uncle." Robin swallowed and nodded. "No wonder you looked familiar! There is a certain likeness to Dad. You don't look like him but there's just something…And I have a half-sister called Julie. An elder half-sister! Feels strange, but exciting!" Derek stood up and said, "Come here, nephew."

Robin rose and walked the short distance towards Derek hesitantly, only to be enveloped in a bear hug. Both men had tears in their eyes as they parted. Derek turned to Susan and said, "Bring out the champagne, Darling. It's not every day that one gains a nephew!"

They marveled at what a small world it was, and how life was full of coincidences.

Robin said, "I'll tell my father tomorrow. Then he can tell Mum. I wonder how she'll take it. She just got to know that her father was someone called Ralph Smith. Now she'll know he's alive and living in the same area as me! But I guess she'll be relieved to know that he didn't leave Granny in the lurch intentionally."

Derek nodded, saying, "I'll go across and see Dad tomorrow. Break it to him gently that Norah has passed on, but he has a daughter. And a grandson right here in Seattle. Once he gets over the shock, I'm sure he'll want to meet you. Are you okay with that?"

Robin nodded and said, "Yes. I'd like to meet him. What about your mother, though? How will she take it?"

Derek said, "No doubt she'll be astonished, but she's essentially a very calm person. And it all happened before Dad and she met. I'm sure she'd like to meet you too."

"Let's see how Mum takes the news. Perhaps we can do a video call with her once she's ready," said Robin.

"One step at a time, Robin," said Derek, patting his nephew's shoulder. "So, do I have any other nephews or nieces?"

Robin replied, "Yes, my younger sister Maya. Would you like to see photographs of her and Mum?"

Derek said eagerly, "Sure. Of your dad too. And your grandmother. I'll show you pictures of your grandfather. Oh, and your cousin, Colin. Our son. He's in college, down in California."

Susan joined them as they took out their phones and showed each other photographs. She looked at them both and thought of the proverb, "Old sins cast long shadows." Well, her father-in-law's "sin," however unintentional, had cast a very long shadow – all the way from India to England, and then to USA. But she was sure that the shadow would lift now, just as it had lifted from his mind, to let joy into his life.

Epilogue
RALPH & JULIE – 2017

Julie held Ralph's arm as they walked up the slight incline towards Norah's grave. As they reached it, she felt Ralph's arm tremble slightly and his step faltered. She squeezed his arm and smiled at him encouragingly.

Julie placed the bouquet of flowers on her mother's grave, then bowed her head and said silently, "Mei, please forgive my father and help him find peace. He was the victim of circumstances, as I'm sure you know now."

She gave Ralph another encouraging smile and stepped back to give him some privacy. She inhaled the pine-scented air and thought of all that had happened since Robin had met Derek, and then Ralph, a year ago. Now, here her father was, at her mother's grave, making his peace.

Back at the cottage, Hallie and Arup were waiting for them. She marveled at how similar those two were – both so calm, sensible, and utterly reliable.

"How lucky Ralph is to have Hallie, and how lucky I am to have Arup!" she thought humbly. "They both love deeply and give unstintingly of themselves to those they love."

She looked at her father standing with his head bowed. After a while, he turned and walked towards her. Their eyes met and there was no need for words. They linked arms and walked in companionable silence back the way they had come.

Outside My Window

Is there another world outside my window?

The Present

Surajit & Indira

I sipped my tea and looked contentedly at the beds of beautiful flowers bordering our lawn. Winter was my favorite season in the tea gardens. I loved planting a variety of flowers and watching them bloom, and relished the fresh seasonal vegetables that came out of our kitchen garden. Winter meant breakfast under a garden umbrella on the lawn, basking in the mild sunshine, feasting our eyes on the beautiful flowers, and watching the butterflies flitting from bloom to bloom. All kinds of birds flew busily around and a chameleon turned red-faced when I caught him watching me through half-closed lids from the bottle-brush tree. I felt blessed to be living amidst all these creatures in such verdant surroundings.

I had lived in a city for a few years only, during my college days and while working for an advertising agency in Kolkata. Then I married Surajit, whom I had known all my life, and came back to the tea estates. Both my father and Surajit's were tea planters too, though retired now. His parents and mine had been good friends ever since I could remember. Surajit was eight years older than me, and had always been the one I'd gone to for advice. He had helped me through adolescence and heartbreak, falling out with friends and all kinds of teenage angst. I trusted him with my secrets, and to his credit, he never laughed to my face, although he did tell me later that he was often tempted to, especially when I behaved as if the world was ending over some small matter.

I could never pinpoint that one moment when I realized I was in love with him. I suppose our relationship just grew and transformed gradually over the years.

When he asked me one day, "So, when are we going to tell the parents?" I didn't even have to ask what he meant.

I glanced across the table at him now, as he held his tea cup and stared absentmindedly at the flowers. Then he turned his gaze on me and smiled. Sometimes he did that across a crowded room, and even after all these years, my heart would skip a beat.

He pushed his chair back from the breakfast table and stood up, walking around the table towards me.

"I'm visiting Kopou today, and having lunch there," he said, referring to one of the tea estates under his stewardship. "So, I'll see you in the evening."

As the General Manager of the tea company he worked for, Surajit was stationed here, at Dobburi Tea Estate, but had to visit all ten estates in turn and report on them.

He bent and gave me a kiss, saying "Bye, Love." Then he patted our dog, Ace, who was snoozing at my feet, before walking swiftly towards the car porch. Ace bounced up and followed him. When Surajit reached the porch, he patted Ace again and sent him running back to me, waved a hand in farewell, and got into the car.

Once the breakfast table had been cleared, I opened my laptop and started writing an article about our recent trip to some Sri Lankan tea estates, for my "tea" blog.

Surajit had been sent on an official visit to a couple of the Nuwara Eliya estates owned by a Sri Lankan tea company, and Surajit's company had kindly allowed me to accompany him.

While in Colombo, we were put up at a historic hotel in the Mount Lavinia area. It stood on a promontory overlooking the ocean, and used to be the Governor General's residence during British rule. Legend had it that a certain Governor General had made a secret passageway which connected the mansion to his gypsy mistress' house. I didn't find out if the secret passage actually existed, but as a writer, I did like the story.

Nuwara Eliya was a few hours' drive from Colombo. It was a very picturesque region, with tea growing on the hill sides. The bungalows were beautiful, and some had spectacular views. The planters and their wives were very warm and hospitable, and I realized that tea planters all around the world share a special camaraderie and sense of brotherhood.

Surajit was especially happy to meet Mr. Gavin Burrows who had been his boss at one time. After his retirement, Mr. Burrows had joined the Sri Lankan tea company as an Adviser. Although based in Colombo, he spent most of his time in the Nuwara Eliya tea estates.

We were pleasantly surprised to meet him at a dinner hosted for us by the Manager of one of the estates.

When Mr. Burrows heard that we were living in the bungalow which had been his residence as General Manager in the late 1970s and early 1980s, he shared some interesting anecdotes. One was about an irate gentleman who had dug holes on the lawn and buried all his wife's clothes when she had left him, but the one that really intrigued me was the story about Mr. Burrows' wife, Margaret, seeing a ghost on the verandah outside the master bedroom – currently occupied by Surajit and me.

"I never believed in ghosts and suchlike myself," said Gavin Burrows to me. "But Margaret was absolutely sure she hadn't dreamed or imagined it. She was a very sensible person. Not given to being fanciful or overly imaginative, but I was skeptical, trying to find a practical explanation. She never told anyone else about the experience, and neither did she bring it up with me again. And then I had that uncanny experience…"

Unfortunately, I didn't get to hear about the uncanny experience because our host interrupted our conversation apologetically, and told us that dinner was served.

Mr. Burrows gallantly escorted me into the dining room and left me in the hands of our gracious hostess. After that, I didn't get a chance to converse with him again.

***

The Recent Past
Gavin & Margaret

Gavin Burrows' grandfather had been a Director of the same tea company that Gavin joined later, and had lived in Calcutta, where the Head Office was located. Gavin's father had been born in Calcutta and spent his early years there before he had been sent to boarding school in England. He continued his education there and stayed back to teach Physics at a college, but took his family to Calcutta once in three years or so, to visit his parents. Gavin had accompanied his grandfather to the tea estates on a couple of those holidays, and fallen in love with the vast expanse of green tea bushes, the smell of freshly manufactured tea, and the whole lifestyle of the tea planter. After his second visit, he knew that the tea plantations were where he would like to spend his life.

By the time he joined the company, his grandfather had retired and returned to England. What most people on the estates didn't know was that Gavin's grandfather had actually owned one-third of the company, and had gifted his shares to Gavin. If he had wanted to, Gavin could have taken his grandfather's place on the company's Board, but he preferred to live and work on the estates. He had requested that no one in Assam be told of his being part-owner of the company. He also insisted that any promotions he was given should be his on merit only.

The HR Director had laughed and said, "I don't think that'll be an issue, Gavin. If you take after your grandfather, which I think you do, you are going to rise pretty swiftly, and solely through merit!" And, so it had turned out.

In the late 1970s and early 1980s, Gavin Burrows was General Manager of the company's ten estates, and stationed at Dobburi Tea Estate.

One summer when Gavin was staying overnight at an estate some distance away, his wife, Margaret, had all the bedroom windows open to let in the breeze. As she tossed and turned, uncomfortable in the summer heat, a welcome gust of wind suddenly blew the curtains apart on the window opening on to the verandah. In the dim light, she saw the silhouette of a woman standing at the window. Jerking upright, she switched on the bedside lamp. Just then the curtains blew apart again, and this time she saw the face of the woman clearly. It was Barbara Hall!

Heart thumping, Margaret's stunned mind tried to make sense of what her eyes had seen.

"Of course, I must've imagined it," she thought. "But why Barbara?"

The wind blew the curtains apart again. This time, Margaret saw Barbara so clearly that she knew she was not hallucinating or imagining things. For a few seconds, the curtains remained apart and Margaret saw the expression of extreme sadness in Barbara's eyes. She also saw the dress Barbara was wearing and recognized it as her favorite day dress in flowered print. Not knowing what to do, Margaret waited, but when the curtains parted again, there was no one at the window.

Margaret lay back, taking deep breaths and waiting for her heartbeat to return to normal. As fear receded, she tried to think rationally. This was the first time in her life that she had seen a ghost, for ghost it was, of that she was sure.

Tom and Barbara Hall had lived in the Dobburi GM's bungalow when Gavin was a young Assistant Manager at a neighboring estate towards the late 1950s. Gavin had brought his bride, Margaret, to the club and introduced her to all the members. Barbara Hall, the General Manager's wife, had been especially kind to the young bride from England who had never been to India before. Over the years, their friendship grew despite their age difference. When Tom Hall retired and returned to Scotland, Gavin and Margaret had tried to meet up with the Halls every time they went home on leave. But when Tom and Barbara divorced and she moved to Italy, they had slowly lost touch. Then they had heard the tragic news that Barbara had committed suicide.

Margaret wondered why she had seen Barbara in Assam when she had died in Italy. "Perhaps she came back to this bungalow because this was where she was happy," she thought. She remembered hearing that suicides couldn't rest in peace. She felt terribly sad for Barbara who had been so kind to her, and wondered if there was something Barbara wanted from her. She couldn't imagine what, but perhaps Barbara would reveal that to her in due course. Slowly, she slipped into a troubled sleep.

The next day, when Gavin returned, she hesitantly told him about her experience the previous night. She wondered if her practical husband would believe her.

As expected, he didn't. Instead, he pronounced, "Indigestion! In future, avoid eating cheese at night," and went off to work.

An indignant Margaret stared after him and called, "But I didn't eat cheese last night!"

She might as well have saved her breath, as Gavin had already bounded down the carpeted stairs.

"And stop running down those stairs! One day you'll fall and hurt yourself!" she called in a louder voice. She had told him this a hundred times before, but to no avail.

Since Gavin hadn't believed that she had actually seen Barbara Hall's ghost, she decided not to tell anyone else about it. Margaret also felt that Barbara may have revealed herself only to her because of their past friendship, so she believed that telling anyone else about the experience might be disloyal to Barbara. She wondered again what Barbara wanted from her. There had to be a reason for her sudden appearance.

It was a few days later that Gavin was bounding down the stairs again. The toe of his boot caught on a small tear in the carpet and he felt himself falling. Clutching at the banister, he suddenly felt a hand hold his arm and jerk him backwards. Instead of falling headlong to the cemented floor below, he found himself sitting on one of the stairs. It all happened so quickly that Gavin couldn't quite understand what had occurred. He thought Margaret had somehow arrested his fall but she was nowhere near him. He looked up and saw her standing at the top of the stairs, staring down at him ashen faced.

"What happened?" she asked, walking quickly down to him.

"I don't know," he said slowly. "One minute I had tripped and was falling down the stairs, and the next I was sitting here."

"I heard you cry out, and rushed to the head of the stairs. I saw you falling, and then suddenly, it looked as if someone arrested your fall and made you sit on that stair."

"Yes, I think that's what happened. I thought it was you but you weren't there," said Gavin.

They looked at each other wordlessly. Then Margaret asked, "Are you hurt? Can you get up?"

"I'm okay," said Gavin. "Just shaken. I'll probably have a few bruises too, but nothing's broken, I think." He took her hand and let her help him up. They walked up the rest of the stairs to the upstairs verandah slowly, and Margaret led him to a chair.

"I've warned you about running down those stairs a hundred times!" she admonished. "Look at what could've happened!"

"Yes, okay, don't fuss, Darling. I'm fine," said Gavin.

"Well, thanks to Providence," said Margaret. "Or was it someone else?" she thought.

Gavin was thinking the same thing. He was a big, tall man, but Barbara had been a strong woman. And anyway, she probably didn't need physical strength now. He looked at Margaret, only to see her watching him.

"What are you thinking?" he asked.

"That Barbara was always a good friend. She liked us both very much, just as we liked her."

He didn't ask her what she meant. He had tried to dismiss the idea of Margaret's seeing Barbara's ghost, but he knew she wasn't normally given to imagining such things. He also knew for sure that someone had saved him from injuring himself badly, perhaps even critically. He had felt the hand closing on his arm and jerking him back.

"Yes, all right. I never believed in the supernatural, but I agree that we can't be sure that spirits don't exist," he conceded.

When Margaret raised her eyebrows, he said in a goaded tone, "Oh, okay. I do believe that you saw Barbara, and it must've been she who saved me just now."

"How do we thank her?" asked Margaret.

Gavin shrugged, saying, "I don't know. Say 'thank you' out loud?"

Seeing Margaret's frown, he hastily added, "I don't know, Darling. This is all outside the realm of my experience. What do you think?"

She thought for a while, then said, "I think we should light a candle for her at the church here and ask the pastor to pray for Barbara to rest in peace. I really can't think of anything else to do to help her." Then added to herself silently, "Unless she appears again and conveys what she wants me to do for her."

When Margaret didn't see Barbara again, she hoped that the prayers at the church had worked, and that her friend had found peace. However, when Gavin retired from the company after several years and took up the job in Sri Lanka, Margaret tried to "talk" to Barbara and tell her that they were leaving.

"I don't know if you're still here. I still don't know what it is you wanted from me. I hope you've found peace, but in case you are still here, I hope you find whatever it is you're looking for. Thank you again, my dear friend, for saving Gavin from what could have been a terrible fall."

***

The Distant Past
Tom & Barbara

Tom Hall's family were ship builders in Aberdeen, Scotland. His great-great-great- grandfather had designed and built some of the fastest clippers which had been used to carry tea from China and India to England. Tom had grown up listening to stories about the excitement caused by the great clipper races, and the way tea clippers had influenced the social norms of the time. To young Tom and his elder brother, Alex, these stories had been magical, especially as they were so closely related to their family. As much as the clippers excited Alex, though, it was the visions of the exotic East – especially India – that excited Tom.

Once he finished school, there was no doubt in Tom's mind about what he wanted to do. His father had died the previous year, and his mother five years before that. His elder brother, Alex, looked after the shipyard. Alex had always loved ships and had studied marine engineering, preparing himself to take over the business one day. Tom had never been interested in ship building, though he liked sailing. He told Alex that he wanted to travel east, to India, and work in the tea estates.

Alex said, "All right, but graduate from college first. That way, if you want to come back, you'll have a better chance of finding a job. Of course, the shipyard is always there for you." Then he added with a grin, "But I know it's not really your cup of tea."

Tom managed to stay in college although his mind was always wandering to the life he hoped to have as a tea planter.

Once he graduated, Alex gave him his blessing, saying, "Go and give it a try."

Tom thought for the umpteenth time how lucky he was to have Alex as his elder brother. He shook his brother's hand warmly, saying, "Thank you, Alex."

Alex returned his handshake just as warmly, and patted his shoulder. "I know someone who works for one of the largest Managing Agents of tea estates in India. I'll give you a letter for him. You can go and meet him in the company's Edinburgh office. They're always looking for adventurous young men like you for their tea estates in India."

A month later, Tom was aboard a ship sailing for Calcutta. On the same ship was a pretty and vivacious young lady called

Barbara Mathews, who was going to spend a few months with her Uncle Bert and Aunt Hilda in Calcutta, where her uncle was a tea broker.

Tom couldn't help but be drawn to Barbara, whose lovely face and vivacity attracted attention from all the unattached men on the ship. Tom had always been a quiet, dreamy young man, quite unaware of how attractive he was to women. He was amazed when Barbara seemed to seek him out and prefer his company to that of any of her other admirers. By the time they reached Calcutta, they were in love.

Tom was met at the docks by a representative of his new employers, while Barbara's uncle and aunt came to receive her. She introduced Tom to them, and he was pleasantly surprised to be invited for supper the next evening. He knew he'd be busy during the day, being briefed about his job and also getting "kitted out" with the clothes he would need on the estate, but was sure he'd be free for supper.

He wanted to propose marriage to Barbara before some young dandy in Calcutta snapped her up while he was tucked away in a remote tea estate in Assam. But he got a rude shock when he read his contract which stipulated that he could not get married until he had completed three years of service. He wasn't sure that it was fair to ask Barbara to wait for him for three years.

They managed to meet a couple more times before he had to leave for Assam, and to his great joy and relief, Barbara agreed to wait three years for him.

"Does that mean we are engaged?" he asked her hesitantly.

"Yes," she replied firmly. "But you'll have to formally ask my father's permission to propose to me when you come home to Scotland next."

"I'll have to do that by letter before I go home, because I want to get married during my next leave. Three years is long enough to wait!"

Barbara promised to tell her parents about him once she returned to England. She and Tom kept in touch through letters which seemed to take an excruciatingly long time to travel from one country to the other!

Tom settled down to life on the tea estate as if he had been born to it. He learned quickly on the job, and even picked up the language of the workers, which was much appreciated. He was a welcome addition to the football teams on the estate and the local club, and started playing golf, at which he soon excelled.

After three years of service, when Tom was given permission to marry, he wrote and asked Barbara's father for her hand in marriage. He also wrote and proposed to Barbara, who accepted. The couple got married when Tom went home on leave, and sailed back to India together.

Barbara loved living on the tea estate. She was interested in growing flowers and vegetables, enjoyed a game of tennis, loved sketching the birds and other creatures that she saw every day, and devoured books borrowed from the club library. She taught their cook to make some staple English bakes and pies, but she and Tom liked simple, non-spicy Indian food too.

When their twin children Robert and Alison were born, they decided to send them to a good boarding school in India once they reached school-going age, rather than send them all the way to Scotland or England. The children loved the school which was up in the hills, and they were always encouraged to invite school friends to spend holidays with them. Once they finished school, Robert and Alison went to college in England.

Tom was excellent at his job, and in due course, was promoted to the post of General Manager. Barbara loved the GM's Bungalow at Dobburi Tea Estate. It had a huge lawn bordered with flower beds which she planted out with a variety and profusion of flowers every winter. She also used every inch of the kitchen garden to plant seasonal vegetables.

Tom and Barbara's Christmas Lunch out on the lawn became a red-letter day on everyone's calendar. They were excellent hosts who made every guest feel welcome.

Lively music played by a band comprising four tea planters set the mood for merriment and dancing, while quantities of beer and pink gins were consumed along with Barbara's special homemade tea wine. Lunch usually comprised roast chicken, mince pie, cold cuts, fresh vegetables from the kitchen garden, salads, steamed pudding with caramel sauce, and a rich Christmas cake. After lunch, the band played Christmas carols while everyone sang along.

Barbara's favorite place in the bungalow was the little verandah just outside the master bedroom. She spent her afternoons there, reading or sketching. She also composed poems, but no one knew that, except Tom. He wasn't what he called "a poetry man" himself, but he thought she expressed herself extremely well, and enjoyed listening to her reciting her compositions. He was also touched by the ones she dedicated to him.

Barbara was well liked because she was friendly and helpful, and had no pretensions although she was the Boss' wife. She made it a point to welcome brides and help them settle down. Tom told her this was invaluable because the quicker the bride settled into her new life, the easier it was for the husband to concentrate on his job.

She admonished him gently, saying, "Really, Tom, all you can think of is work! It's not easy for the girls who come here from England or Scotland. It's a very different lifestyle, and the weather can get very trying, especially the heat."

Tom smiled apologetically and said, "I know, Darling. That's why I appreciate the way you take them under your wing and help them settle down. I'm sure the husbands do too."

The years passed, Robert and Alison got jobs in England, married in due course, and provided Tom and Barbara with a couple of grandchildren each. Soon, it was time for Tom to retire, and after a wonderful farewell party from his company and all their friends, they left India for good. It was an emotional parting from the country and people they had come to love, but they looked forward to spending the rest of their lives close to their children and grandchildren.

While in India, Tom had been busy with work six days of the week and golf on Sundays, while Barbara kept busy with her reading, writing, gardening, wine-making and other hobbies. After retirement, Tom was mostly at home, and while Barbara settled down quickly and kept herself busy with the housework and all her hobbies, he felt at a loose end. Barbara was irritated with his mooching about the house aimlessly, or spending too much time in front of the television. The more irritated she got, the more useless he felt. She tried to be patient but her irritation got the better of her sometimes and she spoke to him quite sharply. To avoid unpleasantness, Tom didn't reply, and Barbara too, decided that it was better to just keep quiet and let him settle down in his own time. As time passed, Tom and Barbara communicated less and less.

And then Tom fell in love with someone else. Clara had been his childhood friend in Aberdeen. They had met off and on when Tom went home to meet his brother while on leave. Usually,

Barbara went to meet her family in Edinburgh at the same time, so she had never met Clara.

Clara had always been secretly in love with Tom, but when he went away to India, and later married Barbara, she married another childhood friend, Davy. She grew to love him deeply, and was devastated when he died of a heart attack at the age of fifty-two.

Clara and Tom bumped into each other in the local grocery store one day, and caught up over coffee. They seemed to bump into each other very often after that, and Tom found that they had a lot to say to each other. Not only did they reminisce about their shared childhood, and Davy, but she also loved to hear about his experiences in India, where she had never been. Tom appreciated her company and reveled in the attention she gave him, but the thought of love hadn't entered his head. Very soon, though, he found himself thinking of her all the time.

"I'm fifty-six years old," he thought. "Too old to fall in love again."

But it seemed that Cupid had no such reservations! When it became clear that Clara felt the same way about him, he knew it was time to talk to Barbara and make a decision.

Barbara was stunned! She had not examined their marriage too closely, but taken it for granted that Tom and she would pull along together for the rest of their lives. When she thought about it, she realized that she still loved Tom. But it was clear that he had moved away from her, and on to someone else. He was apologetic and kind, but firm in his resolve. Since the house was Tom's, inherited from his grandfather, she decided that she should leave. Her sister, Mavis, who had married an Italian, was widowed now, but still lived in Tuscany. She now ran her house in the vineyard as a homestay. When Barbara told Mavis about her impending divorce, Mavis invited her to go live with her and help her run the homestay.

Barbara settled down quite well with Mavis, and, over the years, grew to love the house, vineyard, and Tuscany. Her years of experience in looking after visitors from all over the world as the General Manager's wife helped her in dealing with Mavis' homestay guests. Robert, Alison and their respective families spent holidays with her every year. They gave her news of Tom and Clara, who seemed very happy together. Barbara was glad for them. She had slowly recovered from the shock and grief of losing Tom, and the breakup of their marriage. She realized with regret that she had been insensitive towards Tom, not realizing how difficult it must have been for him to adjust to such a different life.

In Assam, he had been the Boss. Everyone had looked up to him and come to him for advice. He was always busy. Then suddenly he was in Scotland, and a "nobody," with nothing to do.

She wished now that she had been more understanding and given him more time and attention.

It was several years later that she was diagnosed with brain cancer. It was inoperable. After mulling it over, she told Mavis, who was shocked and distressed. So were her children, when she broke the news to them. She even received a phone call from Tom, who was very concerned. He asked if he could do anything to help. She thanked him sincerely and told him there was nothing to be done.

The doctor warned her that there would be increasing pain, and she would have to move into a hospice. She asked the doctor how much time he thought she had. Reluctantly, and with great compassion, he told her she had around six months to a year.

"All right, Doctor. I'll make those count!" she said jauntily, and walked out of his office.

Barbara thought long and hard. She had lived a good life, both in India and Italy. She had spent a great deal of quality time with her children and grandchildren, as well as her dear Mavis. She wanted to leave them at a time of her choosing, instead of becoming a burden to them. She wanted them to remember her the way she had always been – energetic and vivacious. She would make her own plan and not involve anyone else in it. When the time came, she would put the plan in action.

She found her mind wandering back more and more frequently to the happy years she had spent in Assam, specially the last ten years at Dobburi Tea Estate.

"How fortunate I am to have had that wonderful life! I have Tom to thank for providing me with it," she thought gratefully. She could think of Tom quite fondly now. Suddenly determined, she picked up the telephone and called him. She could make out that he was taken aback by her invitation, but after a pause, he thanked her and said he'd discuss it with Clara and get back to her.

They came and spent an enjoyable week with her and Mavis. Barbara made it a point to put Clara at ease.

"It can't have been easy for her to come and meet me, but she made the effort," Barbara told Mavis. "Let's appreciate that. Be kind to her, Mavis."

When it was time to leave, Clara thanked Mavis and then took both Barbara's hands in hers and thanked her warmly. She then got into the taxi, leaving Tom to say his goodbyes. Tom hugged Mavis and thanked her. Then he held Barbara's shoulders and looked at her for a long time. She instinctively knew that, after decades, they were both thinking of that lost life.

At last, he gave her a hug. No words were spoken but they knew that they would not be meeting again. He turned away with suddenly tearful eyes, and walked swiftly to the waiting taxi.

Barbara made a list of all that she had always wanted to do, and started doing them. She made a will, and wrote letters to her children, Mavis, and Tom.

When the first wave of intolerable pain came, Barbara knew it was time to put her plan into action, and she did.

***

The Present

Surajit & Indira

I was intrigued by Gavin Burrows' story about Margaret seeing Barbara Hall's ghost, for reasons of my own. I told Surajit about it once we returned from our trip.

"Do you think Mrs. Burrows really saw Mrs. Hall's ghost, Jit?" I asked him, trying to gauge his belief or disbelief.

"Must've been indigestion like Mr. Burrows said," commented my husband. "Beware of eating cheese at night!" he added, grinning.

"But seriously, Jit, think of all the people who lived here before us," I said. "Their experiences, both happy and sad. What stories this bungalow could tell us if only the walls could speak!"

Surajit smiled indulgently and said, "There goes your writer's imagination! I suppose you're hoping to see a ghost or two yourself so that you can write about them!"

I looked at him and opened my mouth to speak, but just then his mobile phone rang, and the moment was lost. What I was on the point of telling him was that late one evening a few months ago, as I sat writing at my desk which was against the window that looked onto the verandah, I had glanced up and seen a blonde middle-aged woman in a floral print dress looking at me. After a startled moment, I intuitively realized she was an apparition – the first one I'd ever seen. Confused thoughts swirled in my head and my heart thumped in fright, but I still managed to register the deep sadness in the woman's eyes. I realized then that she must've lived in our bungalow in the past. Now, after having heard Mr. Burrows' story, I knew who she was.

A few days later, I was writing at my desk again. Surajit was away for three days, visiting estates some distance away. I lost track of time, and didn't realize that dusk had set in. The curtains were drawn back, and as I looked out onto the small verandah, I saw Barbara Hall again.

This time, however, I had the strangest feeling. I was inside the room looking out of my window, but also outside the window, looking in.

I felt faint and must have blacked out just for a few seconds, because when I opened my eyes, Barbara was still there. We stared at each other, and suddenly memories which I knew were not mine, and yet seemed like they were mine, came rushing into my head.

A lunch party, laughing with a man who was unknown to me, yet clearly my husband. Sitting in the verandah and composing a poem specially for his birthday. Holding the hands of a little blonde girl and a brown-haired boy. A whole kaleidoscope of images swirled around in my head. Then I blacked out again, and this time, when I regained consciousness, Barbara was gone.

I kept sitting in my chair for a few more minutes until I felt stronger. Then I rang the bell and when the Bearer knocked and entered, I asked him to get me a strong, sweet cup of tea.

Sipping the tea, I thought of all those occasions on which I had experienced a sense of déjà vu. I had instinctively known my way around this bungalow from the time we had moved into it. Of course, I had stayed in this bungalow during my holidays from boarding school as a teenager when my father was posted at Dobburi as General Manager, but most of my time had been spent in my room or outdoors. I must have entered the master bedroom occupied by my parents (and now by Surajit and me) of course, but I certainly hadn't known where the secret safe was located. Yet, when Surajit and I had moved in, I had known exactly where it was!

I had memories of a mural painted on one wall of the guest bathroom, just above the bathtub, but when I asked my mother, she insisted there hadn't been one! Then when I asked the household staff about it, one of them looked at me strangely and said it had been there when his father had worked in the bungalow in Mr. Hall's time, but had been painted over many years ago, before my parents' time. I had been baffled then, but now I understood how I had known about the mural.

Then there were some books I had borrowed from the club library. I was sure I hadn't read them before, and yet I had the strange feeling that I had. I remembered now how struck I had been by the fact that Barbara Hall's name had been on the cards of most of the books I had borrowed. In fact, some books hadn't been taken out by anyone else in all the years between her returning them and my borrowing them! In those cards, her name was followed by mine. I got goosebumps now, remembering that.

"So, am I the reincarnation of Barbara Hall, or did she transfer those memories to me telepathically after I moved into this bungalow?" I mused. I felt lightheaded and somewhat disoriented, so I was amazed that I could still think calmly.

"Am I going to tell Jit?" I asked myself. He knew me better than anyone else, but would he believe that what I was experiencing now was real?

Apart from Margaret Burrows, and now myself, I had never heard even a rumor of any other occupant of this bungalow having a supernatural experience. Certainly not my parents, or I would have known.

When Surajit returned, he found me quiet and distracted, and asked me what was wrong. I told him to sit down, then looked straight into his eyes and told him about my experience.

He listened without interrupting, but then quipped, "Did you eat cheese that day?"

I shook him and said, "Don't joke, Jit. It was real, and very disquieting."

He turned serious and said, "Sorry, Love. I'm sure it was very disturbing, and I'm sorry I was away."

"Not your fault," I mumbled. "How were you to know such a thing was going to happen?" Then I added slowly, "In fact, perhaps it was meant to happen in your absence."

He frowned and asked, "What do you mean?"

"Perhaps I had to be alone. Just like Margaret Burrows was alone when **she** saw Barbara's ghost."

He thought about it and said, "According to Mr. Burrows, Margaret never found out what Barbara wanted. Do you have any idea?"

I shook my head, saying, "No."

Surajit looked at me for a while, and then asked hesitantly, "Love, are you sure you saw the ghost? You didn't imagine it, or dream it up, did you? Your creative mind and the power of suggestion…"

I didn't get annoyed. I knew it was difficult for someone like him, or any rational person for that matter, to believe in such things without reservations.

"I'm very sure, Jit," I answered simply but with conviction.

Then I told him about the safe, the mural, and the library books. He looked at me thoughtfully. I could see he wasn't comfortable.

"What do you think all that means?" he asked.

I shrugged, wondering if he guessed the answer but didn't want to accept it.

We didn't get the opportunity to discuss the issue in the next fortnight which was a very busy one for Surajit, taking the company's Chairman around the ten estates. After that, by tacit consent, we didn't discuss it further. That suited me, as I wanted to make sense of the whole experience in my own mind.

It was about a week later that I saw Barbara again. This time, I stared straight at her and asked silently, "What do you want?"

"You know what I want," she replied.

"No, I don't," I said. "How can I, unless you tell me?"

"Because you are me," she said.

"No!" I cried out, "I am **not** you! Stop playing these mind games with me!"

She looked at me with sympathy.

"All right, then. Before my twins were born, I had another baby. A boy. Due to complications during the delivery, he was stillborn. At that time, I was physically weak and so distraught that I never asked Tom where he was buried. I didn't want to know. It was just too painful. I suppose I was in denial. We moved away from the estate soon after that and I pushed his memory to the back of my mind over the years. But now, I can't rest till I know where my child is."

"Tom would know, wouldn't he?" I asked.

"He's passed on, so I can't ask him," Barbara replied.

"Why not? Can't you communicate with him?" I asked curiously.

"No. He's in a different place. He died a natural death, unlike me," she replied.

I understood.

"Which estate were you in, when your baby was born?" I asked.

She told me the name.

"Then why are you here?" I asked. "Why not there?"

"Because **you** are here," was her reply.

"Let's not get into that again, please!" I said hastily.

She shrugged but looked at me with understanding.

"I know this is difficult for you. Believe what you will, but please help me. There's no one else who can do this for me. I tried to tell Margaret, who had been a dear friend, but she wasn't receptive enough. Then I had to wait all these years till you came here, because you and I have a different relationship."

I chose to ignore that but a thought struck me.

"I was here earlier," I reminded her. "With my parents. You didn't approach me then."

"You were too young, so I had to be patient."

"What do you mean? You couldn't have known I'd come back here again!"

She just looked at me steadily, and asked again, "Will you please help me?"

I nodded, feeling sorry for her. I knew what it felt like to lose a child. Surajit and I had lost our first child too. It had been a grief very hard to bear. We had our beloved daughter, of course, but she had her own place in our lives and hearts, and our lost firstborn had his.

"Yes, of course I will. Just give me the details. The year and so on."

After many enquiries and emails flying about among my retired planter friends (my "fan club" as Surajit referred to them, because they all read my blog) we were able to find the little unmarked grave overrun with grass and greenery at the estate Barbara had mentioned.

"What a lonely place," I commented.

Surajit and I exchanged glances as the same thought struck us both. He nodded.

Having gone through the proper channels, we had the remains placed in a brand new coffin and brought little Alexander back with us to Dobburi. We had spoken to our friend Michael Fletcher in New Zealand and asked if he was all right with us burying the little boy next to his father's grave on the river bank.

He was touched that we had asked him, and said, "It's your call, Surajit, but since you ask, I think my father will be glad to have company."

So, after the proper rituals and prayers, Alexander Mathews Hall was laid to rest next to Steve Willis. Surajit and I placed flowers on the little grave. A headstone had been placed with

"Alexander Mathews Hall" and the date of birth and death engraved on it.

I wondered if Barbara was with us, although I hadn't seen her or felt her presence.

"She'll probably come here tonight. I suppose she'll come to me too."

I looked at the river, the trees, the blue sky above, and felt a sense of peace.

As I had expected, I saw Barbara that night. Surajit and I were both asleep but I woke up at around midnight, feeling that someone had called my name. I got out of bed and walked barefoot to the window. I drew back the curtain and saw Barbara standing there. For the first time, she was smiling, and the look of deep sorrow had left her eyes.

"Thank you," I heard the whisper in my head.

I nodded, smiling back.

"So, will you be leaving now?" I asked.

"In a while," she replied evasively.

She smiled again and disappeared.

I padded back to the bed, but as I passed the full-length cheval mirror, I happened to glance at it. The moonlight streaming in through a small gap between two curtains showed my reflection in the mirror quite clearly. Startled, I stopped short.

Were there two reflections? Or was it a trick of the moonlight?

Acknowledgements

There are many people whom I would like to acknowledge and thank.

My parents, Badal and Manju Dasgupta, for giving me the freedom to find my own path in life and encouraging me to treat mistakes as learning opportunities and stepping stones to achievement. I am eternally grateful for their love and support.

My siblings - Rupa, Runi and Anindya - for their steadfast affection and loyalty.

My daughter - Ayesha, and son-in-law - Sidharth, for their belief in my writing prowess and for their loving and unwavering encouragement and support.

My grand-daughter - Tara - for being the treasure that she is.

My husband - Chris - thank you for reading my stories and giving me valuable feedback from a reader's point of view!

My late first husband - Ramanuj - for thirty-three happy and fulfilling years. Those years spent on the tea estates of Assam are the wellspring for the stories in this collection.

My extended family of aunts, uncles, and cousins all across the globe - for the affectionate ties that bind us.

My parents-in-law - Robyn and Bill - for their warmth, bigheartedness, and love.

My step-children - Andrew and Melanie - for their generosity and affection.

My publisher - Michael - for believing that my stories are worth sharing with the world.

My readers - for reading my stories and hopefully, enjoying them.

Thank you!

Sarita Dasgupta